THE QUEENS OF PROPHECY AND POWER

DANIELLE HILL

To all my amazing readers who have stuck with the story till the end, thank you for embarking on this incredible journey with the characters. Your support and love means the world.

Estrella
Caelia
Nix
Kingdom of Soluna
Sale House
Shadow Lands
Estrella

Kingdom of Coldoria
CAELESTIA

GLOSSARY

Word and name pronunciations:

Amara: ah-mar-ah

Avery: eh-ver-ree

Benjamin: Ben-juh-min

Caelestia: kah-lest-ee-ah

Caelia: Kah-lia

Calypso: Kah-lip-so

Chaz: Ch-azz

Coldoria: Cold-or-ee-ah

Cyra: K-eye-rah

Erik: Air-ick

Esmeray: Ez-mer-eye

Estrella: S-tray-ah

Hazel: Haze-ul

Lawrence: Lore-ance

Lola: Low-la

Meresay: Mare-say

Soluna: Sole-loo-nah

Ophiuchus: Oh-few-kiss

Orion: Oh-ryan

Xander: Zand-er

A Brief Recap:

Princess Amara returned from her search for the prophecy after escaping from the Shadow Lands. Prince Xander came to realize the identity of Avery through the picture he found in a journal he stopped Chaz, the Lord of Caelia, from stealing.

Princess Avery was found unconscious after an attack from shadow demons and stuck in the dream-world that she believed to be her real world before coming to Soluna.

Avery then discovered she had even more power with the help of Calypso, and freed herself from the dream-world and regained consciousness. A budding romance ensues between Avery and Prince Xander soon after.

Ben (Avery's friend and bodyguard) finds out Avery true identity and agrees to keep it secret and vows to protect her.

Princess Amara recounts the warning she received from Calypso about trusting no one but herself and they believe someone within the castle is working for the Shadow Lord. Chaz is their prime suspect.

Avery and Amara discover their powers are stronger together. Avery not only has telepathy but also water magic. While Amara has both telekinesis and fire magic. They worked to reinforce the barrier that Amara had placed around the castle.

A guard within the castle is found dead and the castle that is put into lockdown.

After another demon attack, Xander is infected with the same shadowy-poison that killed the guard and many others. Avery is able to save him with a healing ability she did not know she had and does not know how to use.

King Alexander (Prince Xander's father) demands he return to Coldoria. He refuses and instead requests his father send help to aid them from the demon attacks in Soluna.

Amara is kidnapped on her way to meet Avery through the not-so-secret tunnels within the castle. Wesley was the one that took her. Earlier when she returned form the Shadow Lands, her and Lawrence concluded that time moves slower in the Shadow Lands than it does in the rest of Caelestia.

Amara figured she had enough time to save her best friend, Wesley, and the rest of the Celestials trapped in the Shadow Lands. However, the Shadow Lord warped the frame of time once more, making it faster now than it is in Caelestia.

The castle was once again attacked by shadow demons that were now even stronger than before, allowing them to take on a more physical form than the ones they're encountered in the past.

While the fight raged on, Avery was cornered by Esmeray (Calypso's evil doppelganger) who had actually been Vivian (Chaz's wife) all along.

She exposes how Ben had been unwillingly working for her and feeding her information. She would wipe his memory every time so he would remain unaware.

Esmeray kills Chaz and then orders Ben to kill Avery under the influence of her shadow magic. Ben ends up killing himself to save Avery. Esmeray amused by this decides to prolong taking Avery, and vanishes alongside the demons.

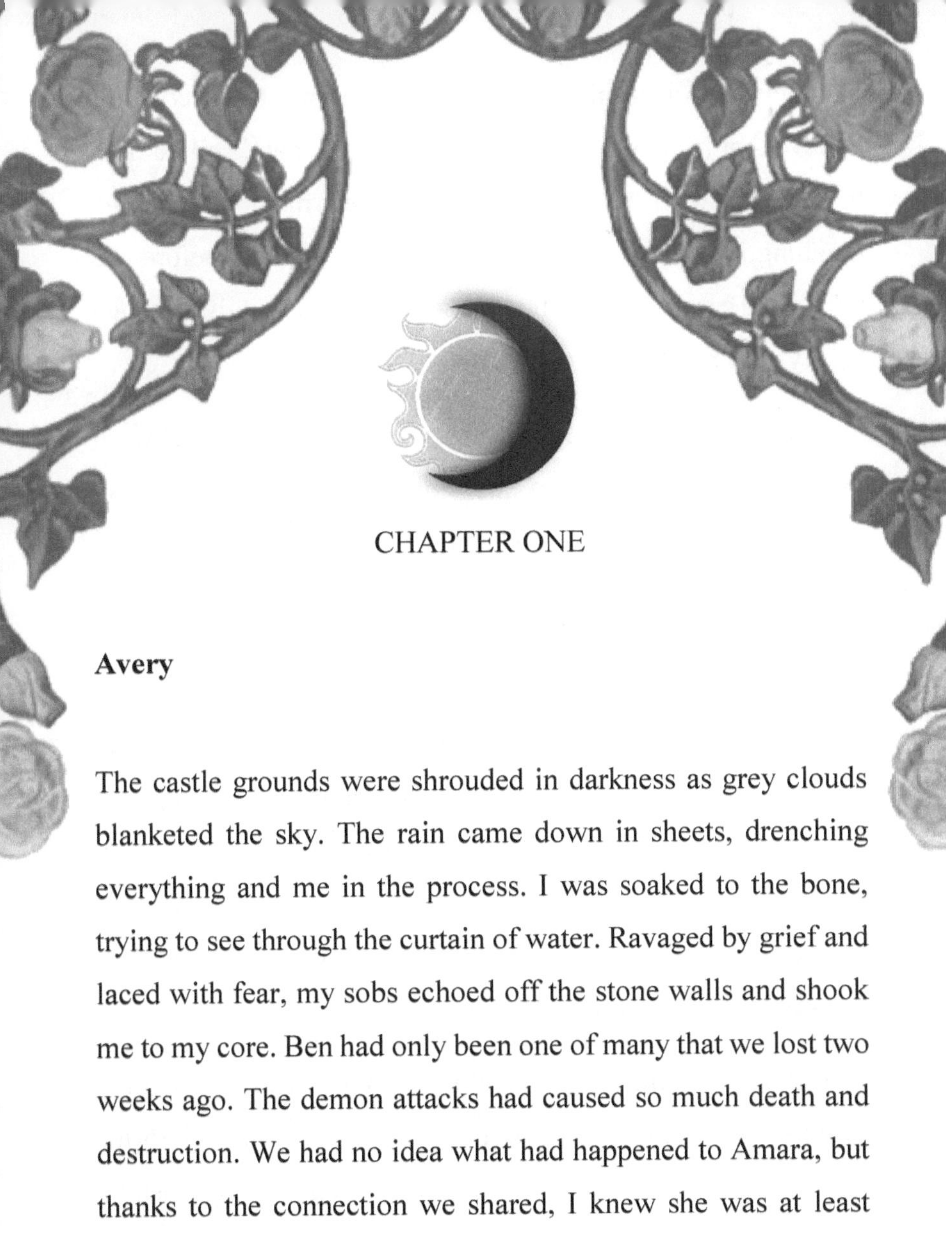

CHAPTER ONE

Avery

The castle grounds were shrouded in darkness as grey clouds blanketed the sky. The rain came down in sheets, drenching everything and me in the process. I was soaked to the bone, trying to see through the curtain of water. Ravaged by grief and laced with fear, my sobs echoed off the stone walls and shook me to my core. Ben had only been one of many that we lost two weeks ago. The demon attacks had caused so much death and destruction. We had no idea what had happened to Amara, but thanks to the connection we shared, I knew she was at least alive, wherever she was.

I trudged through the castle gardens, my gaze eventually settling on the memorial bench placed under the tall willow tree. My legs quivered when I saw Ben's name engraved on the shiny plaque along the backrest. The guilt had once again consumed me; Ben had given his own life to save mine. I still couldn't believe that he was gone. Tears brimmed over and spilled onto my cheeks as I recalled all our shared memories here—laughing, talking, reading, and writing. I kneeled before the bench and carefully laid a bouquet of flowers, lovingly arranged by my own hands.

Taking a deep breath, I closed my eyes and let the grief wash over me. The memory of his smile stung; he was always smiling. Tears continued to stream down my face.

"I miss you, Ben. Thank you for saving my life. I will never forget you," I whispered.

No matter how hard I tried, the guilt continued to linger within me. Every time I shut my eyes, I could see Ben's joyful expression turn into that empty stare as he took his last breath. But I knew that he would have wanted me to be brave and move forward—he had done what he did for that very reason. Yet, try as I might, I just couldn't bring myself to do it.

Instead, I sat motionless on the bench, my heart threatening to burst through my chest as I watched despairingly into the garden, replaying every moment. The weight of it crushing down on me. What could I have done differently? Could I have saved him? If I were just a little bit stronger, would I have been able to fight off Esmeray's control over my own body? It didn't matter now because it was too late; my inaction had sealed his fate. A chill ran down my spine at the thought of something like that happening again.

A young woman materialized before me like a ghost. Her pale face was so much like my own, with light freckles scattered beneath her emerald eyes that pierced right into my soul. Her silver hair shone like a beacon of moonlight, illuminating everything around her.

My body trembled with anticipation as I whispered, "Calypso?" into the heavy rain. Blinking away my tears, I could hardly believe it when she appeared before me. She shimmered like a mirage in the downpour, her dreamlike presence almost too beautiful to be real. She inched closer, and I looked around, desperate for something or someone to tell me if this was really happening. But there was nothing but the stormy night, with no one else in sight. With my heart pounding in my chest, I gasped, "Are you really here?"

"Your power is getting stronger," her voice sang out to me, but her lips didn't move.

"But not strong enough," I mumbled, the regret and anguish of losing Ben piercing me just as deeply as they had just moments before.

"Shine your light and illuminate the world." The melody of her voice resonated, seeming like so much more than just words being spoken.

"What does that mean?" I demanded, shoving myself to my feet. My fists clenched as I stepped toward her, anger and confusion surging within me. She didn't move or say a word; she just looked at me with a calm expression. I was still unsure if this were really happening; it had to be some sort of vision, didn't it?

"Do not lose sight of your main focus. Remember, your presence is the key to vanquishing the shadows that plague this land."

"But how?" I shouted, my arms flying up in frustration.

"Shine your light," she said before she vanished completely.

"Ugh!" I screamed, kicking the mud, before I collapsed to the ground. My knees smacked against the soggy earth with a dull thud as the cold moisture consumed me.

Burying my face in my hands, I sobbed. For Ben, for everyone else we had lost and would probably lose, for Amara, and for the fear and uncertainty of what lay ahead.

The sound of soft, squelching footsteps in the rain-soaked grass reached me, growing louder as they approached. I raised my head to see who it was. Xander. He wore a long black raincoat that had been pulled over his head to protect himself from the downpour. In his arms, he held what I had initially thought was a blanket, but as he got closer, I realized it was a black velvet hooded cloak.

The moment he draped the soft cloak around me, I felt the heat radiating from his body from where his hands brushed against my arms. He knelt beside me and pulled me into an embrace. His heart pounded quickly against my ear as I sobbed uncontrollably into his chest. He tenderly ran his fingers through my hair. His warm body contrasted sharply with the chill of the night air that had seeped through my clothes. He didn't speak; he just held me.

An eternity seemed to have passed in the silence, every breath aching with sorrow. I sobbed and gasped until there were no more tears to be shed, yet still, the pain remained. Until finally, his voice spoke through my torment like an agonizing knife, slicing away at the remnants of my grief.

"Are you ready?" he asked gently, his blue-green eyes searching mine for assurance. I swallowed hard and nodded, unconsciously gripping the folds of my tattered, mud-soaked gown. "The citizens of Soluna are waiting for their queen to explain everything," he reminded me. Taking a deep breath, I stood, feeling the heavy weight of responsibility pressing down on my shoulders.

We were fortunate that the castle was cleared of people before the demons arrived. Still, there was no denying what now seemed inevitable. Those who had seen the destruction firsthand quickly spread word of it throughout Soluna. Everywhere we went, there were whispers of fear and dread.

Xander wrapped his strong arm around my waist and held me steady as we walked through the gardens. I shivered once we stepped inside the castle, grateful for the added warmth after being out in the rain for too long. Soft light spilled down from ornate lanterns strung along the walls, casting the corridors in a faint golden glow. Our footsteps echoed off the stone floors.

The walk back to my room was a blur, aside from the fact that Xander guided me every step of the way. He looked at me with an intensity I couldn't understand.

His mouth opened and closed, and my brow quirked up as I shot him a questioning look. His lips twitched slightly as he said, "I guess it's a good thing I helped you overcome your fear of heights since you will be speaking to your people from the top of the watch towers of the castle gates."

I groaned and lightly shoved him away, suppressing a chuckle. "You didn't exactly ease my nerves. But thanks for the reminder that I'm terrified."

Xander smirked as I pushed past him and stepped into my room.

My hair and clothes were caked in mud. I couldn't believe it had come to this. I never wanted to be a princess, let alone a queen. But there I was, about to address the people of this kingdom, pretending to be someone I wasn't. The hot shower did little to ease the tension in my body as I thought about what was coming.

As I dried myself off and dressed, I could feel the weight of the crown on my head. A physical reminder of the responsibility that came with this role. One mistake could cost many lives. It already had.

Xander and Lawrence, flanked by an intimidating force of royal guards, stood like statues before my bedroom door. As I emerged, they all bowed in unison, with Xander offering his arm to escort me. Lawrence moved in next to Xander, his gaze shifting between us as if he was expecting something else to happen. The royal guards fell into formation behind us, their armour glinting in the candlelight. I felt an overwhelming weight as their presence trailed behind me, every eye on my back.

We hadn't passed another soul as we made our way towards the watchtower. Lawrence had warned me that practically every citizen in and around the castle would be in attendance and that I would need to soothe the crowd. The sound of my heart pounding in my chest grew louder with each step I took up the winding staircase towards the tower.

My mind raced, running through a million different scenarios of what I should say, still not making a decision on what to do when I reached the top. The air seemed thick with dread as I stepped onto the platform. I was glad that the rain had at least stopped.

The citizens had gathered in the castle courtyard, ready to hear their queen's explanation. I could feel their eyes on me, their expectant faces illuminated by the wavering flames of torches.

The fear was palpable, like an electric charge in the air. Beads of sweat formed on my forehead as I started to explain what had happened to Ben. Eyes widened and lips parted;

everyone was listening intently as the realization of how real this was hit them.

I took a deep breath to steady my nerves. My voice shook at first, but then grew stronger as I found my footing.

"I stand before you today in the wake of this tragedy. Our kingdom has faced a darkness unlike any other, and we have lost so much. But I want to assure you that we will not lose hope. We will not let the shadows win."

CHAPTER TWO

Xander

The moonlight shone down as if it were specifically made to highlight her, almost as if it had been summoned to honour the loss of life that surrounded her. A dark veil of sorrow was cast over the grounds as the families of those tragically taken too soon gathered to pay their respects. Standing tall with her chin raised, she looked not only like a queen but a goddess, the gentle gust of wind billowing her long golden hair as well as the skirts of her long, dark gown.

"My beloved people, the demons have struck, but we will not be defeated. We will not let their evil actions break our spirit or our unity. Instead, we will stand strong together and honour the memories of those we have lost. Let us take comfort in the fact that they will live on in our hearts and in the stories we tell. We will not forget them, and we will continue to fight for a better future for all. May their souls rest in peace, and may we find the strength to move forward together as we fight back and rebuild what has been destroyed."

The silence seemed to stretch on forever as I waited with bated breath for the crowd to respond. True grief was shown through her beautiful words, and I wasn't the only one to have noticed. Suddenly, a single soldier that stood with us on the watchtower began yelling "Long Live the Queen!" which quickly spread throughout the entire crowd like wildfire. As one, the people below shouted their love for her. My throat constricted as I uttered those same words of reverence. I could feel my entire being filled with admiration for the woman who stood before me.

A thunderous roar shook the earth and echoed through the crowd of mourners. "Stop!" a male voice bellowed out, reverberating off every surface with complete authority. A man strode through the parted mourners. He wore a deep blue cloak and a gold breastplate emblazoned with the Solunian royal crest. His presence was commanding and regal. Shock and awe rippled through the masses as they realized who stood before them. Silence filled the air as he declared again, "The true king has arrived." It was Chaz Ashburn, Duke of Caelia. The Queen's soldiers stepped forward, swords drawn and ready.

Avery's eyes widened in disbelief as she stumbled backward. My hand shot up instinctively, landing on the small of her back, steadying her. The Duke shouldn't have been here. Avery had told me about how she had witnessed his death that night. So how was he standing there now, claiming to be the true king?

He clenched his fist and pointed to where Avery stood, his voice booming in accusation. "She is not the real Princess Amara; she is an imposter!" he roared. "She is under the influence of the shadows and will lead you all to ruin!" His words echoed across the space as everyone stared in shock at Avery, her expression contorted with fear.

My hand slowly moved from Avery's back, sliding down her arm until our fingers were tightly intertwined. I gave her a gentle yet firm squeeze, a silent assurance that I wouldn't leave her alone to face Chaz's relentless claims. Despite my comfort, she didn't move. I wondered if it was because of the shock of seeing Chaz, his words that brought up painful memories from that fateful night, or everything combined. The murmurs of the crowd grew louder and more critical as their doubts and suspicions threatened to undo all of the progress she had made here.

Chaz spat out the words with contempt, his face twisted in a sneer. His fists clenched at his sides as he went on. "The imposter murdered my wife in cold blood—the same fate that would have befallen me had I not been locked away in the dungeons."

The citizens below erupted into horrified gasps filled with despair and confusion. Avery's hand trembled in mine. Her complexion had become even more pale than usual; her eyes were wide with shock and began to water. I knew I had to act fast.

A fire of determination blazed in my veins as I took a protective step in front of Avery, hoping to shield her from their judgment. My eyes burned with an inner light as I stared out into the crowd, whose faces contorted with doubt. I spoke with a depth of conviction that could have shaken the very tower we stood on. "She is no imposter. She is the rightful heir to the throne of Soluna—and my future wife."

Erik, Hazel, and even Vic were quick to support my claims as they shouted their agreements from where they stood below at the front of the crowd.

The Duke of Caelia was quick to counter. He slowly turned his head, and for a moment the silence was deafening before he shouted up to me, "Your claims have no base!" He waved his arm dramatically towards my friends and family. "The four guests from Coldoria have spent too much time in the presence of the imposter; she has bewitched them with her dark magic!"

Lawrence's face was stern as he stepped forward, hands clenched at his sides. He spoke in a deep and commanding voice, delivering his words like a hammer strike. "Do not believe the lies of this traitor to the crown! His treason has been an abomination, and he should still be locked away in dungeons."

The murmurs of the crowd increased in volume, ricocheting off the stone walls. Unsure of who and what to believe.

As I reached for Avery's hand, her gaze suddenly shifted away from me and towards Lawrence. Her body tensed, and her knuckles turned white as she gripped my fingers tightly for a moment before releasing them. Taking a deep breath, she stepped forward resolutely with determination written across her face, the calming caress of the moonlight highlighting her silhouette. Reaching into her skirt pocket, she pulled out a tiny silver orb that shone like a star and seemed to pulse in time with her heartbeat. She had told me how it spoke to her—a soothing feminine voice reciting an ancient prophecy—on one of those sleepless nights when memories of what had happened in Amara's room kept haunting her.

She placed her free hand on Lawrence, and he bowed before gesturing for her to take the place where he had stood.

A hush fell over the group as she spoke, her voice almost ethereal. "Only the one involved in the prophecy, the *true* heir to the throne of Soluna, can wield it."

"See! Sorcery!" The duke's voice called, refusing to give up.

As they observed Avery and the orb, the onlookers' expressions changed from curiosity to wonder. I just couldn't allow him to dampen their adoration with his skepticism any longer. I strode forward, stopping only a step behind Avery and slightly to her side so that everyone could marvel at the sight before them. "Coldoria has an alliance with Soluna and will continue to uphold it only with its rightful heir next in line for the crown, my queen." With that declaration, I fell onto one knee, my hand placed over my heart, feeling the chill of the stone floor through my clothing.

A hush descended upon the gathering as each person slowly got down on one knee and bowed in reverence to Avery, recognizing her as their queen, and I just prayed it stayed that way.

The guards finally marched towards the duke, who stood tall amidst everyone else. Two of them seized his arms firmly, while four more surrounded him in defence, and they escorted him away.

CHAPTER THREE

Avery

Prince Xander's steady presence provided a semblance of security as he escorted me back through the grand corridors of the palace. The weight of recent events hung heavy in the air, and the urgency of our situation was palpable. The plans and preparations for the impending journey back to Coldoria to secure reinforcements were already in motion. Xander was taking both Erik and Vic with him.

Hazel's fate took a different turn. She was to remain in Soluna with me. Their father was still under the impression that she was in Alden with Lord Sterling, and we didn't want that to change. Her presence was comforting to my aching heart, a respite from the isolation that threatened to consume me.

The morning after the attack, Xander had told Hazel and the others about me and Amara—of our identities and what was at stake. I wasn't thrilled, but it was better than living in constant fear of being exposed. It felt good to have someone else know what was really happening. They made a pact to keep our secret safe, and I believed them.

The impending departures of Xander, Erik, and Vic cast a sense of urgency over our discussions. They needed to pack and ensure everything was ready. As the others made their way towards the door, Xander stood before me, placing a soft kiss on my cheek. My eyes held his, a silent promise passing between us, but I wasn't exactly sure what it was.

"I'll come find you before I leave," he vowed, and then caught up with the others.

Once the throne room doors closed behind them, a feeling of responsibility settled on Lawrence and me as we faced the mysterious disappearance of Amara. The missing pieces in the puzzle of her whereabouts hung over our heads like a dark cloud. Lawrence's furrowed brows mirrored my own inner turmoil.

"This isn't like her. Not in a time like this." Lawrence's voice carried a mixture of determination and concern.

"We'll find her," I promised, though we both knew I could do no such thing. Uncertainty clawed at the edges of my resolve. The path ahead was shrouded in darkness, and assurances were hopeless.

He watched me for a moment before speaking. "You should take another sleeping broth."

I nodded in agreement, acknowledging the wisdom in his counsel. I needed to rest; we both knew that. I hadn't had a normal sleep without the broth since that night. Every time I closed my eyes, my mind seemed to replay Ben's death. In the solitude of my room, the outside world fell away, leaving me alone with the haunting memories of his face as I held him.

Lawrence had walked me back to my room and waited with me until the castle healers had brought me the sleeping broth. It sat on the nightstand next to me as I sat at the edge of the large bed. The steam and smell of the broth filled my senses. I still hadn't taken it. I would, just not yet.

As the night deepened, the stars outside my window bore witness to the turmoil within. The kingdom was on the brink of chaos with Chaz's unexpected return, and our problems were far from over. He was supposed to be dead; I *saw* him die. Xander was leaving, and I didn't know what would happen next. The spectre of uncertainty cast a shadow on our path. In the midst of everything that was going on, the mystery of Amara's disappearance lingered.

Though exhaustion pulled at me, my mind was too busy to rest. Desperate for a distraction, I pulled on a cloak and headed out into the night. My steps carried me to the stables, where Amara and I used to train together.

With a deep breath of conviction, I attempted to recreate the same shield around the castle grounds that had once protected us with its pale golden light. But no matter how hard I tried, it wouldn't work. As more time passed, it was clear that this skill was beyond my reach; no matter how hard I tried, the delicate threads of power eluded me like grains of sand in an hourglass. I wasn't strong enough to do it alone. I needed her.

Coming to terms with my new reality, my eyes were drawn to the water trough nearby, as if it inspired me to explore the depths of this other power I held within. Closing my eyes, I tapped into my internal reservoir and reached out to the element around me. With a single thought, the water stirred and rose against gravity's power. It obeyed my commands like an extension of myself.

As I willed, the water around me became solid and began to form into something almost human. There was no mistaking the humanoid quality of its blurred features. The form's physical proof of just how much my progress and power were improving.

Spikes of ice suddenly emerged from their hands, breathtakingly dangerous as they gleamed in the faint moonlight that shone in from the cracks in the roof of the old stables. I led them like a conductor with a baton, and our movements together created a mesmerizing ballet of power, control, elegance, and deadly intent.

I was immersed in my concentration when I felt the familiar presence of Xander approaching. His footsteps were light and graceful. I looked up to find him standing before me, admiration glimmering in his eyes.

"Impressive," he said, jerking his head toward the water creatures I'd created.

As if to counteract how stunning they were, my head whirled back toward them just as their shape collapsed and the water splashed the ground, showering us in the process.

I blinked in response, turning back to Xander. The corners of his mouth twitched into a small smile.

"Practice makes… progress." I shrugged.

"Just progress? I'd say it's a lot more than that. You're growing stronger every day."

"Not strong enough," my gaze fixed on my wet feet as I muttered to myself under my breath, but he heard. Of course he heard.

He closed the distance between us, his hand cupping my chin as he tilted my head up so my eyes met his. "I mean it."

I nodded, unsure of what else to even say. I didn't want to argue; I knew my power was getting stronger. But it couldn't change the past. I just hoped it would be strong enough to save the rest of the people I cared about.

His relaxed expression quickly changed to one of duty and responsibility, serving as a reminder of the reason he had come looking for me.

"We depart for Coldoria in an hour," he declared.

His hand found mine, the warmth of his skin and the strength of his grip sending a shiver through me. We left the stables together and entered the castle gardens. The stars glimmered above us, each one twinkling brighter than the last.

Our steps were in sync. The connection between Xander and I took another turn as he leaned in, his breath warming my neck just before his lips met mine. Our skin practically sizzled with anticipation, and passion ignited between us. He pulled me closer, our hands roaming each other's bodies. The world around us faded, and all that remained were our hearts beating in time with each other.

Time melted away, the embrace of pleasure intertwined with tendrils of fatigue. Grogginess seeped in, pulling at my consciousness, half-asleep and half-aware. Xander's strong muscles cradled me as he carried me from the gardens. The gentle rhythm of his heart from where my head rested on his chest made it even more difficult to stay awake. With care, he carried me back to my room, the one I had once shared with Amara.

He settled me in, his touch soft and affectionate. A kiss was pressed against my forehead, and his voice had a soothing melody. "Rest well, love," he murmured.

As sleep claimed me, I felt safe in his presence. The trials that awaited us were still present in my mind, but for this brief moment, I found comfort in the safety of dreams for the first time since that night.

CHAPTER FOUR

Amara

The cold, damp embrace of the dungeon welcomed me as I was unceremoniously cast into its depths. The torchlight barely penetrated the gloom, casting eerie shadows that danced on the walls like sinister specters. Though the cold, dark, and dripping dungeon weren't the best of accommodations, they were not the most pressing issues on my mind.

Rats, beady-eyed and relentless, scurried along the edges of my confinement, their company a stark reminder of the isolation that had become my daily existence. In this abyss, they were my companions, far more innocent than the shadow demons that lurked beyond the bars, their malevolent presence serving as jail wardens to my prisoner.

A mirthless chuckle escaped my lips at the thought of losing my sanity to the clutches of isolation. However, the chilling wails that reverberated throughout the dungeon silenced any glimmer of amusement. Celestials, stripped of their powers, their mournful cries echoed through the air, a haunting symphony of despair.

My arms were tightly bound to the iron cuffs affixed to the cold, damp stone wall. Wearing only a thin nightshirt, I shivered from the chill of the air and the fatigue that seemed to sap my energy. It had been too long since I'd last seen sunlight; the darkness was only broken by the candle perched atop a wooden barrel in the corner of the cell. Its feeble light illuminating the chamber pot, a humiliating necessity, its putrid smell enough to make me gag.

I closed my eyes in an attempt to block out the haunting wails and piercing cries that seemed to follow me even in my dreams. Exhaustion tugged at every fibre of my being, and I was finally forced to surrender to sleep's embrace.

An ethereal call seemed to enter my mind from within some sort of distorted dream where reality and illusion intertwined. In the depths of my unconsciousness, a familiar voice called out, faint yet unmistakable. My sister's soul reached out to me, a beacon in the darkness.

A pull, a magnetic force, guided me.

My voice trembled as I shouted Avery's name, the sound echoing through my mind. I felt like I was calling to her from some otherworldly realm, desperate for her and our words to cross the divide between us.

The air began to thicken, and without warning, the walls of our reality were pierced, and we found ourselves in an underground chamber. The smooth stone walls were exquisitely adorned with intricate paintings and carvings, depicting ancient Sun and Moon worshippers in mid-ritual. An altar intricately carved with pillars rose at one end.

A sob ripped from Avery's throat as we embraced. I could feel her chest heaving; every gasp was an agonizing reminder of the pain my disappearance must have caused. "Amara," she whispered brokenly, "where are you?" The anguish in her voice was unspoken yet undeniable—the depth of her suffering was rumbling between us in this shared moment of grief.

I clutched her by the shoulders, our gazes locked together. I gulped air as if any moment I might be plunged again into the darkness that had threatened to consume me. "I was betrayed," I said, voice shaking, my throat tight with suppressed fury. "Wesley…he…he imprisoned me in the Shadow Lands."

Avery's expression twisted, a complex interplay of shock, anger, and pain. She deserved to know the truth, even if it meant sharing the depths of my ordeal. "Are you sure?" Her voice carried a mixture of disbelief and rage. Though she had never met him, I had told her about him and what he had meant to me.

I nodded, my gaze never leaving her. "Yes." My voice wavered, the guilt of my absence an unspoken burden.

Avery's eyes softened, a mix of compassion and understanding. "Amara, you can't blame yourself for—"

Her words were cut short as the dungeon's thick, iron door groaned as it swung inward, and a hulking shadow engulfed the space.

She was gone, and I was back inside the dungeon.

Wesley stepped inside with measured strides, his imposing presence filling the space. Now that the warmth he had always given me was gone, being in his presence was like being stabbed by a frigid knife.

"Well, well, if it isn't the lost princess herself," Wesley sneered, his words laced with a mocking tone. "Such a shame no one even knows you're missing." The corners of his mouth curving into a sinister smile.

I wove my words carefully, hoping to reach the remnants of humanity within him. The man who had always been there for me. The man I loved. My best friend. "Wesley, there's still good in you. You don't have to continue down this path of darkness," I pleaded.

He scoffed, bitterness tainting his expression. "Good? Any good I had died when you left me here to rot."

I was at a loss for words. My heart heaved in my chest, and tears welled up in my eyes as his sharp words sank in. I wanted to scream that it wasn't my choice. That *he* was the one to force me to leave him here, but the words stuck in my throat. All I could think of was how much I didn't want to go.

"No matter what I did, it was never good enough for you!" he shouted, a wild and maniacal gleam in his eye. A sneer twisted his lips as his hands flew out to point at me, bound and constrained by chains. He let out a bitter laugh that echoed through the room, reverberating against the cold stone walls. "Well, look at you now."

A sob escaped my lips as I frantically shook my head. "No! You were *too* good for me. This isn't right; this isn't you!"

"Oh, but it is. This is what happened once you abandoned me here. I desperately held onto hope that you'd return for me. I waited for so long—for years—for you to return. But you never came back. The things they did… the pain they put me through while my heart kept hoping... Now you'll feel a fraction of the pain I endured in your absence."

"Years? Wes, what are you talking about?"

"This is what my love for you did to me. So, I stopped fighting against what the Shadow Lord wanted. I yielded to her wishes. And she rewarded me with unbelievable power."

"She?" I asked. "Wesley, who is the Shadow Lord?"

He smirked. "Esmeray, the true queen."

"Wesley, I—"

My words were silenced as a storm of rage exploded from within him, a tempest that he unleashed on me. In an instant, the room transformed, shadows coalescing into serpentine forms, slithering and hissing, a reflection of my deepest fears.

The shadowy snakes were coiling and tightening around my throat until I felt unable to breathe. Panic lodged in my chest as I gasped for air, but the pressure only increased.

Pain surged as they sunk their illusory fangs into my mind. They finally loosened their grip around my neck, and I screamed, not only from the agony of their assault but from the realization that Wesley had slipped further into the darkness than I could have imagined. His malevolence had taken a darker turn, and it was a darkness that threatened to consume us both.

CHAPTER FIVE

Xander

Leaving Avery's room, a sense of both relief and yearning lingered within me. Her form, now nestled in the comfort of sleep, eased the worries that had plagued my thoughts. But that yearning—the longing for her presence, for her touch—was a flame that refused to be extinguished. With a soft exhale, I turned away from her door, my steps guided by duty, purpose, and the promise of what lay ahead.

I tapped my knuckles lightly against Hazel's door before slowly opening it. As I stepped through the threshold of Hazel's chambers, a wave of warmth washed over me, radiating from the hearth on the far side of the room. She looked up at me, her eyes widening as a spark of happiness filled them.

"Xander, you're here," she exclaimed as her little smile lit up her entire face.

Crossing the room, I pulled her into a tight embrace. "Of course," I murmured, my voice carrying a mixture of affection and protectiveness. "I couldn't leave without saying goodbye to my little sister."

Her arms tightened around me, and I felt her heartbeat against my chest. "Promise me you'll come back," she whispered, her voice tinged with worry.

I pulled back slightly, my eyes locking with hers, silently conveying a sense of solemn assurance. "I promise. I'll be back before you know it."

A smile touched her lips, but her eyes held a hint of sadness. "Just...promise you'll be careful."

"I will," I vowed. "Keep an eye out for Avery, and make sure you take care of yourself too."

Her eyes a combination of determination and vulnerability as she nodded. With one final squeeze of her hand, I left her chambers, my heart heavy yet resolute.

Meeting up with Victoria and Erik, I found them ready and waiting, their horses pawing at the ground in anticipation. Alongside them were two Solunian guards, chosen by Lawrence for their skills in horsemanship and their loyalty.

As I swung myself onto my horse, a rush of exhilaration surged through my veins, electrifying my senses and serving as a powerful reminder of the formidable challenge that awaited me.

"Are we all set?" I called out, my voice filled with determination and urgency.

Victoria nodded, her expression focused. "Ready and waiting."

Erik chimed in, his voice laced with a playful undertone. "And my charm is ready to shine on this journey."

Vic rolled her eyes while I snorted a laugh. "Let's hope that charm doesn't get us into too much trouble."

The horses' hooves clicked against the cobblestone streets. The wind carried a sense of anticipation, teasing at our clothes and hair as we rode faster than any carriage could take us. I glanced over at Erik, who rode by my side. His eyes were fixed straight ahead—his determination strong and unwavering. We rode on, following the twists and turns of the city as we raced towards our goal.

As the city's outskirts gave way to open terrain, my thoughts drifted inward. Our mission would be wrought with difficulty, and I wasn't sure how far we could go or what kind of future awaited us. My father's rule was powerful and unyielding. I knew he would never do as I asked and help Soluna. So, I was ready to challenge his authority and bravely carve a new way forward that put both kingdoms' needs before all else.

As my heart beat in time with my horse's powerful strides, I knew that I was prepared for whatever lay ahead. The loyal hearts that beat alongside me, supporting me, were the foundation upon which change would be built.

42

CHAPTER SIX

Avery

I jolted awake, gasping for air, as the final echoes of Amara's voice resonated in my consciousness. A connection that should have been impossible was now a terrifying reality—I had seen into her thoughts and felt the desperation of her sorrow. Her words revealed a truth so devastatingly dark that even the dreamworld couldn't contain it. A chill ran down my spine as I realized this could not be a mere dream.

I quickly got out of bed, pulling on my clothes as I headed towards the door. My mind raced as I tried to make sense of what had just happened. *How could I have seen into Amara's mind like that? Was it even real?*

As I reached the hallway, I realized something was off. The usually bustling castle was eerily quiet, with only the sound of my own footsteps echoing off the stone walls. I walked cautiously, feeling as if I was being watched.

Turning a corner, I came face-to-face with a hooded figure. My heart leaped into my throat as I tried to scream, but no sound escaped my lips. The figure reached out a hand towards me, its boney fingers almost touching my face.

And then I woke up, sweating and panting. It had been a nightmare, one that felt so real that it took me a moment to realize it wasn't. I took deep breaths, trying to calm myself down, before getting up.

Gathering my courage, I stumbled out of bed and forced myself towards Lawrence's study. My heart felt heavy with the memories of last night, Amara's words echoing in my mind.

With my hand on the doorknob, I hesitated momentarily before slowly stepping inside. His usually pristine clothing was dishevelled and his hair slightly unkempt, as though he had been running his hands through it nervously. He sat slumped in the chair, his head cradled in his hands. Despite the darkness cloaking the study, I glimpsed a shattered expression and traces of exhaustion. He lifted his gaze at my entrance, his lips curled into an effortful smile that didn't quite reach his tired eyes.

"Lawrence, what happened?" I asked, my voice laced with worry. Something was definitely wrong. I doubted he had seen the same thing I had last night, but it was clear something had happened.

He waved me off, a gesture that seemed forced. "Just a bad night, Avery. Nothing to worry about." My skepticism must have shown across my face. Once his eyes met mine, he let out a resigned sigh. "I suppose I cannot hide things from you, can I?"

I raised an eyebrow, shrugging one shoulder. "I could literally read your mind if I wanted to, though it would be a huge invasion of privacy, and I am trying to only use that gift when necessary." I admitted.

He rubbed his temples, a sigh escaping him once again. "You're right. It's Liliana. I've been having nightmares about her." His admission caught me off guard—a realization that Lawrence's worries ran deeper than I had imagined.

"Nightmares? About your sister?" I asked gently. He nodded curtly in response.

"It started a few weeks ago," he began. "At first, they were just flashes of her face that would appear in my dreams and vanish just as quickly. But lately, the dreams have become more vivid; some of them even feel real enough for me to reach out and touch her." He paused for a moment before continuing, voice thick with emotion.

My heart ached at the vulnerability in his voice, the weight of his fears revealed. "Lawrence, you can't blame yourself for—"

He shook his head, his eyes hollow. "It's as if my mind is haunted. I know better than to fall for the tricks and manipulations of the shadows, but these nightmares... they feel real."

He took a deep breath before continuing.

"Different scenarios, different ways she's... she's in danger. Begging me to save her, blaming me for what happened to her." His voice was barely above a whisper now. I felt helpless at seeing Lawrence so raw and exposed, struggling with such intense emotions yet unable to help.

"I'm sure Liliana would never blame you," I said quietly, placing my hand over his. He looked up at me then, his eyes filled with sorrow and guilt that I could feel radiating from him like waves of heat.

"Maybe," he said softly. But even though his lips curled into something resembling a smile, I knew he still hadn't forgiven himself for what happened all those years ago with Liliana.

I had wanted to tell Lawrence about the connection Amara and I shared in my dreams, but I was now filled with doubt. Uncertainty clouded my judgment, and I began to question the reality of what I'd seen. *Should I tell him or keep it to myself, at least for now?*

Our conversation shifted, and I realized I would wait to tell him about my dream, Amara, and the Shadow Lands.

He informed me of a new guard assigned to my protection—one to replace Ben. The mention of Ben's name was like a knife to my heart, and every time I thought about his death, I was overwhelmed with grief and remorse.

As he was relaying this information, a frantic guard burst into the room. "Your Highness, Lord Lawrence, the capital, Estrella is under attack!"

The guard's announcement broke through our conversation, cutting the air with a sharp urgency. Lawrence and I exchanged a look of disbelief before he rose to his feet, immediately alert.

"What do you mean Estrella is under attack? Who is attacking it?" Lawrence demanded, his voice hard and commanding as he strode towards the guard.

The man inhaled deeply before speaking, his words tumbling out in a rush. "We don't know yet."

We hurried into the corridor and were swept into the chaos. Guards shouted orders at each other, swords clinking against their armour in a desperate melody. Nobles weaved through the mayhem as they searched for a place to hide.

Lawrence's booming voice echoed off the walls, commanding someone to fetch horses at once with no argument or hesitation.

Hazel rounded the corner, her eyes widening in fear as they met mine. "What's going on?" she exclaimed, her chest heaving with panic.

"Hazel, stay here. The castle isn't being attacked," I shouted as I made my way towards her.

"But I want to help!" The fear in her voice was mixed with a strong resolve.

I placed a hand on her shoulder, my gaze unwavering. "I know you want to help, but it's too dangerous."

"Oh, but it's fine for you to go?" She practically threw my hand off of her. "I'm going with you."

"We don't have time to argue about it," I pleaded with her, hoping she would just drop it.

Her eyes narrowed, telling me she wouldn't let it go. I grabbed the arm of a guard as she was passing by, stopping her.

Once she realized who I was, she bowed deeply. "How can I help, Your Highness?" she asked.

"I need you to escort Princess Hazel back to her chambers and ensure she is safe until we return." I tried not to look at Hazel; I knew the glare in her eyes would be enough to make me regret this request. "Use force if you have to."

The guard nodded before turning towards Hazel. Hazel tried to pull away, but the guard's grip was too strong, and she practically dragged her through the hallway. I held my breath as they disappeared around the corner, praying that Hazel wouldn't be too much for the guard to handle.

The air was heavy with a sense of dread as we made our way to the capital. I shivered, despite the warmth of my cloak. A group of royal guards, some on horseback and others on foot, joined Lawrence and me.

The scene before us was one of pure chaos. Demons, their movements wild and frenzied, tore through the streets with an unrelenting ferocity. Cries of terror mingled with the scent of smoke and blood as magic sizzled in the air.

Lawrence shouted orders at his men, issuing instructions with a clarity that could not be questioned. The men obeyed without hesitation, forming a circle around us as we made our way deeper into the city.

We encountered several demons along the way, but Lawrence's orders were swift and decisive as he dispatched them with practiced ease, leaving nothing but dust in their wake.

We continued forward until we reached the heart of the city, where chaos reigned supreme. Demons ran wild among humans in a chaotic dance of destruction, tearing through everything in their path without mercy or remorse.

Around us lay carnage and death, yet somehow life still found ways to persist: scared citizens huddled together for protection while brave soldiers charged into battle against impossible odds.

As we galloped across the cobbled streets, I spotted an ethereal woman standing amidst the chaos—with long silver hair that flowed freely in the wind, her figure framed by an orange-tinted sky.

I recognized her immediately.

It was Calypso.

I jumped off my horse as I ran towards her, feeling as though no one else could see her. She had something to show me, something to tell me. Without hesitation, I continued running wildly towards her.

"Princess! Wait!" Lawrence shouted desperately from behind me, trying frantically to get through the throng of demons that blocked his path. But I would not be stopped.

As I finally reached her, she spoke words that were meant only for me: "Shine your light and illuminate the world."

CHAPTER SEVEN

Avery

Calypso faded away, her cryptic words still echoing in my mind. I whirled around to see Lawrence and the guards fighting off hordes of demons. Taking a deep breath, I focused on Calypso's message: *Shine your light and illuminate the world.*

My hands burned with silver energy that erupted from me like a tidal wave, washing over half of the demons and slowing the rest down. As the magic coursed through me, I felt a tug inside myself and commanded my water beings to attack what demons remained. They grew vicious spikes that slashed and ripped into the creatures as my silver glow cut them down one by one until there were none left.

The aftermath of the demon attack was devastating. Everywhere I looked, broken bodies and destroyed buildings were strewn about like discarded toys in a playground. There was no sound but that of our own heavy breathing as we all stood in shock at the carnage before us.

I shook my head to clear my thoughts and shouted out to the dumbfounded citizens, reminding them of the dangers at hand and that they should get to safety—preferably somewhere far away from here. To the guards, I issued orders to check around the city for any other attacks or people in need; we couldn't leave anyone behind.

Lawrence had quickly regained his composure after his initial shock subsided and began herding everyone together before leading them away from the scene with determined strides. As we followed him through the streets and alleyways of Estrella.

My low voice carried barely above a whisper as I hurried alongside Lawrence. "We need to get any injured survivors back to the infirmary at the castle," I said, my eyes flicking between Lawrence and our surroundings.

Lawrence nodded, his eyes scanning the area for any signs of danger. "Agreed. But we need to make sure it's safe first. We don't know if there are any demons still lurking around."

My mind raced with possibilities. "I can use my water beings to scout ahead and see if there are any threats."

Lawrence looked at me with surprise but quickly recovered. "Very well, do it. But be careful, Avery. We can't afford to lose you."

With a nod, I closed my eyes and reached out with my mind to my water beings. They shrank down in size, slithering out of the puddles and drains, flowing through the street like a river. They scouted ahead; their senses heightened to detect any danger.

After a few tense minutes, my water beings returned with the all clear. I relayed the message to Lawrence, and we continued on, keeping our guard up and our weapons at the ready.

As we approached the castle grounds, I could see the black marks on the walls and hear the glass crunching beneath my feet. Guards patrolled every corner of the property, swords drawn and arms tensely crossed in front of their bodies. My heart was hammering in my chest as we entered the palace gates, but a wave of relief swept over me when I saw that it had withstood the attack.

I quickly made my way to the infirmary, where healers were bustling around carrying bandages and herbs while tending to dozens of wounded citizens.

The sounds of shouting and voices raised in fear echoed down the corridor, and I raced out to investigate. Around the corner from the Grand Hall, I could make out individual words like 'protest' and 'outrage'. Chaz was standing tall at the front, his authoritative voice cutting through the chaos.

The crowd had grown restless and angry, clamouring for explanations regarding the identity of the otherworldly figures that had fought against the demons. Chaz, seeing an opportunity to seize control of the kingdom, stepped forward.

"People of Soluna!" he shouted in a commanding tone. "You are all doomed to death and damnation if you do not make me king! Only I can protect you against these enemies! Make me king, and I shall grant you safety and security!"

"How?" I was seething with rage, pushing my way through the crowd, determined to reach the front. I climbed up onto the stage, glaring at him. "How can you possibly protect this kingdom better than me?" I shouted, emphasizing every word. "Those water nymphs helped fight the demons that attacked." I finally gave a name to the water beings I created.

The crowd around us murmured in agreement, clearly voicing their support for me over Chaz. However, some still seemed as though they wanted to believe him.

He frowned and shifted uncomfortably from one foot to another before finally speaking up again. "Your Highness, while your bravery is admirable," he almost laughed, "it is not enough to ensure the long-term safety of this kingdom." We need someone who is willing to think strategically and make hard choices when necessary—someone who has experience in leading large groups of people through tumultuous times." He paused for a moment and looked out at the crowd before continuing, "And that person is me."

I boiled with anger at his audacity. "You had nothing to do with defeating the demons. You're just trying to exploit this situation to gain power for yourself. You don't care about Soluna. You only care about yourself."

The crowd was now completely on my side, shouting their agreement and support for me. Chaz scoffed; his face was red with anger and embarrassment, and he sputtered for a moment before finally speaking again. "Fine! If you don't believe I can lead this kingdom, then maybe I'll just have to take it for myself!"

With that, he turned and stormed out of the Grand Hall, a few of his followers trailing behind him.

Taking a deep breath, I turned to the rest of the crowd and spoke with a calm, clear voice that carried throughout the hall. "My dear citizens, I understand that you are afraid and angry. But we must not let fear and anger cloud our judgment. The Duke of Caelia is not the answer. He only seeks to divide us and turn us against each other." I exhaled, feeling the adrenaline slowly leave my body. "We must stand together as one, united against the true threat that looms ahead. The demons will not stop until they have destroyed everything we hold dear. But we will not let them. We will fight back with everything we have. And we will emerge victorious."

The crowd erupted into applause, cheers, and cries of support as they began to disperse, feeling reassured and hopeful. I stayed behind, listening to their chatter and making sure everyone was okay. It was clear that the people trusted me, and

I would do everything in my power to protect them and the kingdom from any threats that might come our way.

As the last of the crowd left, I glanced up at the ceiling and whispered, "Calypso, you're right. I will shine my light and illuminate the world."

The sound of footsteps approaching had me turning swiftly to find the source, praying it wasn't Chaz coming back. It wasn't.

It was Lawrence, his eyes filled with concern. "Are you alright? That was quite the speech."

I nodded, a small smile on my lips. "I'm fine. Just needed to remind them of what we're fighting for."

I paced within Lawrence's study. We needed to discuss some things and decided it would be best not to do it out in the open.

Lawrence leaned against his desk, his gaze fixed on me, which held both familiarity and reservation. "Avery," he began, and I stopped my pacing to look at him. "I've been giving much thought to the curse that plagues Soluna."

"What about it?" I asked.

He sighed, a weight settling in his words. "The citizens of Soluna have now witnessed magic firsthand, something unlike any of the other small magics we see on the daily, yet their minds remain shrouded in ignorance about its existence before the curse."

I wasn't exactly sure why Lawrence was bringing this up. We knew the curse affected people's minds. It was the whole point of the curse. "Do you think there is a way to undo the curse?"

"I don't know. But I am hoping that once we defeat Shadow Lord—defeat Esmeray—the curse will also be broken."

My thoughts shifted to Chaz, remembering how Esmeray had killed him. She had been disguised as his wife, Vivian. Did Vivian ever even really exist? Or was it all part of some bigger plan? "What about Chaz? Do you think he might hold some of these answers?"

Lawrence's expression tightened. "The duke is a mystery, Avery. You saw him fall at Esmeray's hands. Yet here he is."

"Could it be some kind of illusion or trick? We already know that Esmeray can take many different forms. Could she be impersonating Chaz?" I asked with uncertainty but was hopeful that this could have been it.

"Might be," Lawrence replied thoughtfully. "Or perhaps some other type of dark, sinister magic." His eyes shifted to the old spell books that belonged to his sister on his shelf. "Your powers... they seem to be growing."

I nodded, though he never took his eyes away from those books.

His voice was soft when he spoke again. "Just promise me you'll be careful. This world of magic is treacherous, and the shadows can be deceiving."

"I promise," I vowed, my voice carrying the weight of determination. "I won't ever let the shadows get me."

The guards had found Chaz lurking around the corridors by my chambers and brought him back to the dungeons. We weren't sure how he kept escaping, but I figured it was time I paid him a visit.

As I walked through the dungeon's dark, damp corridors, I could feel my heart racing with anticipation. Chaz had been a thorn in my side for too long, and I was determined to get some answers from him.

Chaz was sitting on a rickety bed, staring off into space. His expression was a mixture of anger, frustration, and defeat. When he saw me, he narrowed his eyes and scowled.

"What do you want, *Your Highness?*" He spat out.

I ignored his hostility and approached the bars of his cell. "I want to know how you're still here. I saw Esmeray kill you."

Chaz sneered at me. "You're not as smart as you think you are, Princess. Maybe you should ask yourself why Esmeray spared your life when she could have easily killed you."

The implication hit me like a ton of bricks. "Are you saying that I have something to do with your resurrection?"

Chaz chuckled darkly. "No, but you are part of a bigger plan, Princess. You and your precious kingdom are just pawns in a game that has been going on for centuries. And I'm afraid you're not on the winning side."

I felt a chill run down my spine at his words, but I refused to show any fear. "What game? What are you talking about?"

Chaz leaned forward, his eyes flashing a crimson red. "The game of power, Princess. The game of the gods. You see, there are forces in this world that are beyond your comprehension."

"Maybe I know more than you think I do. But I'm not here to talk to you about what I know; I want to know what *you* know." I gritted my teeth, frustration building inside of me.

Chaz leaned back against the wall, a smirk playing on his lips. "Believe what you will, Princess. But mark my words, the game is already in motion."

"Tell me everything you know about Esmeray," I demanded, my voice firm.

Chaz raised an eyebrow. "Why should I? You don't exactly have any leverage over me."

I couldn't deny that he was right. I had no power over him, especially not locked up in a cell—a cell he kept somehow escaping from, no doubt with the help of Esmeray.

Chaz let out a bitter laugh. "Oh, you mean the Shadow Lord? What could I possibly tell you that you don't already know?"

For starters, Esmeray *is* Shadow Lord. I fought to hide my surprise; I had my suspicions after her reveal, but this confirmed it.

Chaz's smirk grew into a full-blown grin, and he let out an eerie chuckle. "Esmeray is not someone you want to mess with, Princess. She is powerful, cunning, and ruthless. She's been around for centuries, and she's not about to give up her power anytime soon."

I narrowed my eyes, trying to suppress the fear that was creeping up my spine. "What is she after? What does she want?"

He only shrugged, his eyes glowing that eerie red colour.

"She really did kill you, didn't she? That wasn't a trick or illusion." I whispered.

Chaz's grin faded, replaced by a haunted look. "She did. But death is not always permanent. Not when you're dealing with dark magic."

My mind raced with the implications of his words. Was Esmeray truly immortal? Did she have some sort of spell to bring back the dead? And why was she so interested in Soluna? I had so many questions, but Chaz wasn't offering any answers.

I took a step back from his cell, feeling a sense of unease wash over me. "I don't know what kind of game you're playing, Chaz. But I'm going to find out the truth, one way or another."

Chaz chuckled darkly. "Good luck with that, Avery. You're going to need it."

As I walked away from his cell, I couldn't shake the feeling that Chaz knew something I didn't. Something crucial about the game that was being played in the shadows.

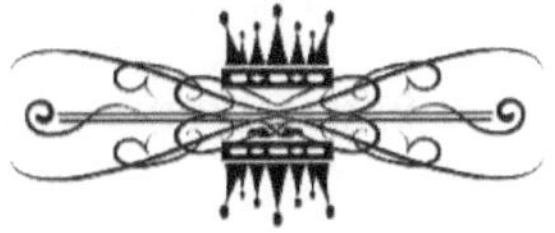

There was one more person I knew I needed to pay a visit to today. The heavy weight of guilt pressed down on me as I made my way to Hazel's chambers. I allowed the guard to practically drag her away. I knew it was for her own safety, but I knew I would have felt betrayed if the roles had been reversed. As I approached her door, I was filled with an urgent need to apologize.

I hesitated for a moment, my hand poised to knock, before finally rapping my knuckles against the ornate wooden door. The shuffle of footsteps echoed from inside, and the door creaked open to reveal the guard from earlier.

She stood in the doorway with her fists clenched around the hilt of her sword, ready to defend Hazel, if need be, but recognition quickly crossed her face, and she stepped aside, allowing me to enter. Her shoulders relaxed as I passed, and the door shut behind us with a soft click.

I took a few tentative steps into the room, keeping my gaze averted from Hazel. I could feel her eyes burning into me, and I knew that she was glaring daggers my way. I cleared my throat and forced myself to look at her. "Hazel, I... I need to apologize." I said meekly.

Hazel didn't say anything right away, but her expression softened slightly. She shifted her position on the bed and finally looked up at me. "You have nothing to be sorry for," she said in a small voice.

I opened my mouth to protest, but she held up one hand with a sigh. "Avery, you did what you thought was best for both of us—and for your mission as a whole. You wanted to protect me from the dangers of those *things*… and the same goes for you too. We both did what we had to do, and there's no use dwelling on it now; we need to focus on finding a way out of this mess."

My shoulders fell with relief as a weight lifted from my chest at hearing those words—words that meant more than just an apology accepted—words that meant understanding and forgiveness.

"Thank you, Hazel. I really am sorry, though," I whispered softly.

The palace guard, who had been standing quietly in the corner of the room, cleared her throat, a subtle reminder of her presence. "Your Highness, I will be stationed just outside the room. If you need anything, don't hesitate to call."

"Thank you." I nodded, relieved for the privacy.

Hazel and I settled onto a pair of plush chairs. I eyed the platter of food sitting on the table between us; however, neither of us touched anything.

She fidgeted with her hands as she looked at me, her eyes full of concern. "How worried are you about Xander?" she asked, her voice trembling slightly.

"I can't help but worry," I admitted. "The demons that attacked Soluna... they could have reached Xander and the others before they even made it to Coldoria, or they could be in danger there too."

Hazel nodded, understanding the gravity of the situation. "I'm worried too. If he's in trouble, we need to help."

"But how?"

Hazel leaned back in her chair, crossing her arms over her chest. "I might be able to help with that at least. I have contacts in Coldoria who can at least tell us if they've been under attack."

I raised an eyebrow in surprise. "Really? How would we be able to get a message there before Xander? He has already left—anyone else we send will get there after him and be putting themselves at risk too."

"Not if we send a falcon." The corner of her lip tipped up.

"A falcon?" I repeated.

"Yes, our kingdoms have used them many times to send messages. This could work!" The hope in her voice shined.

"Okay, well clearly, I don't know anything about that. So, you should go find Lawrence; he'll know and help." I grinned at her, impressed by her resourcefulness.

Hazel returned the smile, grateful for my encouragement. "Thank you, Avery. I'll go find him now."

As she stood up to leave, I reached out and grabbed her hand. "Hazel, thank you for understanding. I never meant to hurt you or make you feel like I didn't trust you."

"I know," she said, squeezing my hand reassuringly. "We're in this together, Avery. We'll find a way to save Soluna and everyone we care about."

With that, she pulled her hand away and left the room, leaving me alone with my thoughts. The weight of the world was still heavy on my shoulders, but I was glad to still have Hazel here with me.

I stepped out of her room to find the guard still standing at attention outside the door. "You didn't follow Hazel?" I asked in disbelief, glancing up and down the hallway for any sign of her.

She bowed low as she spoke. "Forgive me, Your Highness, but I have actually been ordered to be your new personal guard."

She was Ben's replacement. I thought, and I only nodded, unable to trust any words that might have come out.

The guard bowed again before she spoke. "My name is Larina, Your Highness. I will do whatever I need to do to protect you."

Her words reminded me so much of similar ones Ben had spoken to me. I would not cry. I would not let anyone in the castle see me shed any more tears. I needed to make it back to my room.

I dipped my chin in response to Larina's words, still too overwhelmed for words. I felt the tears pricking at my eyes once more as I thought of Ben and all he had done for me. I blinked them back quickly, not wanting anyone in the castle to see me cry.

Turning away from Larina, I started walking down the hallway, my feet feeling heavy and slow with each step. It didn't feel right to have someone else follow so close behind, but I couldn't bring myself to tell her to walk by my side like I had with Ben.

I thanked Larina before heading into my room for the night, and she had assured me she would be stationed just outside if I needed anything.

Once inside my room, I immediately collapsed into bed and let out a deep sigh of relief. This was the only place where I could be alone with my thoughts and memories. I thought of Ben. Of Amara and whether or not she was truly in the Shadow Lands. And I thought of Xander, praying that he was okay.

Maybe Amara will contact me in my dreams. Assuming it was real. I wondered as my mind began to drift off into sleep.

CHAPTER EIGHT

Amara

Days blurred into nights as I was trapped in a haze of darkness and despair. I had no way to tell how long I had been stuck in this nightmare, an abyss where time moved faster, stealing away the seconds like a thief in the night.

Esmeray had been a constant visitor to my cell; her cruel smile was a haunting reflection of my torment. She sought to unravel the depths of my powers, to probe my mind, and to assess the boundaries of my strength. The pain she inflicted upon me came in waves, a relentless assault on both body and soul.

As I hung by a thread, teetering on the precipice of sanity, I couldn't help but wonder if resistance was futile. The allure of surrender, of yielding to the power of the shadows, whispered seductively in the darkest corners of my mind. But the memory of Avery, her face etched with despair as she fought the shadow-infused version of myself, served as a stark reminder of the consequences of such a choice.

And then there was Wesley; he had betrayed me and now walked in Esmeray's shadow. His presence in this forsaken place made me question the worth of my defiance. Bitterness threatened to consume me, but I refused to let the darkness define my path.

I found solace in my dreams—visions that kept me connected to those I loved and reminded me why I kept fighting.

"Wesley," I pleaded, desperation dripping like acid off my tongue. "How could you do this to someone you claimed you loved?"

I couldn't see him, but I could feel his presence lurking in the shadows, observing me silently. His laughter erupted like shards of broken glass, cutting into my soul with every mocking cackle he uttered. "Love? You were nothing more than a weakness, Amara, an inconvenience. Ophiuchus is the one who truly understands me and has saved me from myself."

The revelation hit me like a ton of bricks. Ophiuchus had been working with Esmeray from the very beginning. Had the entire rebellion here been a lie?

As I stared into Wesley's dark eyes, I no longer saw the softness they once held for me. With renewed determination, I whispered, "Wesley, I'll save you from her grasp, just as I'll save myself."

He chuckled, "Good luck with that."

But I refused to let his words discourage me. I closed my eyes and focused on my powers, reaching deep within myself to find the strength I needed to break free from this prison.

Suddenly, the air around me grew colder, and I shivered as the icy gusts of wind whipped my hair around my face. The room somehow seemed even darker than before, with the shadows seeming to come alive.

This wasn't my magic. It was his.

Wesley stepped before me, and I could feel the shadowy tendrils leaving his body and snaking up around mine. My eyes widened as they tightened their grip around me, threatening to consume me in their darkness. But I refused to succumb to fear.

Drawing on strength from deep within, I reached out with my own magic and pushed against the shadows attempting to take hold of me. Instead of retreating, however, Wesley's shadows seemed to grow more powerful, swirling around us both like a tornado of darkness. I felt like I was suffocating—the air had become thick with their presence.

The tendrils wrapped around my neck like a snake, tightening with the same deadly intent. My vision began to dim as I looked into Wesley's nearly black eyes, narrowed with sinister glee at the fate he had in store for me. Struggling for air, I could barely whisper his name.

"Wes," I gasped, my voice cracking under the pressure of his dark magic.

Just when it seemed all hope was lost, an unexpected ally joined the fray. A brilliant light shone through the darkness, illuminating both Wesley and myself in its glow. A voice echoed from within the light—Calypso's voice—calling out for us both to be freed from Esmeray's grasp.

Wesley's shadows immediately retreated, snaking back into his body before dissipating entirely. His face softened as he looked at me sadly before turning away without a word.

My relief was short-lived; however, as moments later, Esmeray appeared before us with a smug expression on her face. Clearly, she had been watching the entire time.

"Congratulations, Amara," she purred, her eyes glinting with malice. "It seems you're more powerful than I gave you credit for. You think you can break free from my grasp?" She laughed tauntingly.

I tensed, bracing myself for whatever torture she had in store for me. But to my surprise, she turned away and left. I was left both relieved and confused. The heavy door of the cell clanged shut as she stalked away, echoing off the dank walls until all that remained was silence.

Exhaustion took over my body, and before I knew it, I was in the same dream-like world as before. In front of me stood Avery, a silver light radiating off of her.

"Amara," she said softly. "Is it really you?" Her eyes were wide with disbelief and hope.

I sighed with relief, grateful to see my sister's face once more. "Yes, it's me," I whispered. "How are you? How's the kingdom?"

The joy seemed to fade from her face as she shook her head. "I've been trying to reach you again. I wasn't sure if what I'd seen last time was real or not."

"It was real. I'm in the Shadow Lands—I have to get out of here, Avery. I can't take much more of this."

Avery swallowed hard, looking around nervously. "I don't even know how to get to you."

"Ask Lawrence about an old safe house—I discovered it in our mother's journals. He should know about it." My pulse quickened at the thought of freedom, but I reminded her not to go alone. "There is a tunnel underneath the safe house I found through the library; follow it. The Shadow Lands has a protective barrier around it," I said carefully. "But there's something telling me that she'll let you in—just make sure you're not alone."

Avery nodded, determination evident in her gaze. "I won't be alone, Amara. And we'll get you out of there, I promise."

Tears threatened to spill down my cheeks, and I could feel the weight of my exhaustion bearing down on me. "Thank you, Avery. I don't know how much longer I can hold on."

"Just hold on. We'll be there soon."

With those words, the dream faded, and I was alone once more in my cell. But for the first time in what felt like forever, there was a glimmer of hope in my heart. Avery was coming for me, and together, we would find a way out of the Shadow Lands.

CHAPTER NINE

Avery

There was a slight but persistent shaking that disturbed my sleep. In the hazy moments between sleep and wakefulness, I lashed out instinctively, swatting away the intrusion with a groan of annoyance. But as my eyes slowly adjusted to the light and my mind became slightly less clouded, I realized that it was Hazel.

"Avery, wake up," she whispered urgently, her voice a soft plea.

Blinking away the remnants of sleep, the world gradually came back into focus. The warmth of my bed clung to me like a comforting cocoon—one I never wanted to leave—and I couldn't help the irritation that washed over me. I turned to Hazel, ready to scream my annoyance at her, but then I noticed the apology in her eyes.

"I'm sorry for waking you, Avery," she said, her voice tinged with guilt. "But we need to talk."

My heart sank as different scenarios raced through my mind; nothing good ever came after 'we need to talk.' "Is it Xander? Is he okay?" I swung my legs over the edge of the bed, facing Hazel where she stood.

She took a deep breath, her words rushing out in a torrent of explanation. "It's Lawrence; he is not doing well. I went to see him, and he is convinced that things will only get worse. We were able to send out two letters with the falcons. One to Xander and one to my contact in Coldoria. But we are unsure if Xander will receive his; we know the other will reach Coldoria soon."

My chest constricted with worry, the weight of our kingdom's uncertainty pressing down on me. "We can only hope it reaches them soon and can only wait until we hear back. I'm sorry, Hazel. I know this must be so hard for you."

"For you, too," she countered. "I know you and my brother are... well, whatever you are, I know you care about each other."

"We do." I agreed.

Hazel gave me a sad smile. Reaching out, she clasped my hand in hers. "Then we'll get through this together," she promised.

I squeezed her hand back, appreciative of her support. "Thank you, Hazel. You're a good friend."

She didn't say anything back; her gaze fixed on a spot on the floor between us. For a moment, we both just sat there in silence, lost in our own thoughts. The weight of the situation hanging heavily in the air. But then, as if on cue, Hazel's typical excitement returned. "On a lighter note, though, I have to tell you about your new guard, Larina."

I couldn't help but chuckle at the sudden change in topic. "Oh? What's she like?"

Hazel's eyes lit up with a mischievous gleam, and her lips quirked into a smirk. "She's cute, Avery, really cute. But she's also infuriating. She *actually* dragged me out of the Great Hall in front of so many people. It was embarrassing—thanks again for that," she said with an exaggerated roll of her eyes and a teasing reminder that it was done on my orders. "She's so rude and emotionless."

Hazel's voice rose louder and higher as she spoke, emphasizing each of her points against my new guard. As I listened to her tirade, I couldn't help but chuckle at the situations she described—the tension in the room quickly melted away until we were both laughing.

"She's so overzealous in her duties," Hazel said between laughs. "It's almost as if she takes pleasure in dragging me around."

I smiled in amusement, shaking my head at the thought of what a formidable pair they would make. "Why don't you two just get along? It could be beneficial for both of you."

Hazel shrugged, her expression thoughtful. "I guess I should try to make an effort," she said slowly. "She was only following orders after all. Plus, as I mentioned, she's stunning."

The comment was so unexpected that it made me laugh again. "Really? I think the word you used was cute, then infuriating, and now stunning. So, which one is it?" I teased.

"She can be all of those things at once," she replied defensively, but then her lips twitched into a small grin.

Just then, there was a soft knock on the door, and Larina's voice carried through the wooden barrier. "Your Highnesses, I've had some honey tea prepared for you. It may help with your nerves."

I struggled to suppress a smile as I whispered playfully to Hazel, "Oh yeah, she seems so emotionless and infuriating."

Hazel let out an embarrassed giggle before quickly composing herself—she wasn't one to be caught off guard by a guard. She opened the door and stepped aside to allow Larina in.

Larina bowed her head before stepping forward with a tray of steaming honey tea, two mugs, and what looked like some type of biscuit, which she set down on the table in the sitting area. She stood at attention with her hands clasped behind her back, as if expecting me to issue an order for her next move.

But instead, I just took one of the mugs from the tray and gestured for Hazel to do the same. "Thank you, Larina; why don't you join us?" I gestured to the love seat while I took the only chair intended for one person to sit on.

"Oh, thank you, Your Highness," Larina said as she sat down.

Hazel shot me a death glare behind Larina's back before dropping into the empty spot next to her while I laughed quietly into my mug. As I took a sip of my own drink, the sweet honey flavour was just what I needed, and I fought the urge to groan.

"I hope the tea is soothing," Larina said, her voice shaking as her eyes darted between the two of us. I doubted she was used to sitting around drinking tea with two princesses.

"It's wonderful; would you like some? I can have someone bring us another cup—"

"No! I mean… No, thank you; I couldn't... I'm working," she stuttered.

"You can't have a tea break?" I suggested.

Larina shook her head adamantly. "It's not proper for me to indulge in such luxuries while on duty," she replied.

I raised an eyebrow at her response. "Well, I disagree. I think it's important for you to take care of yourself while you're working. You can't do your job if you're not feeling well or overworked."

Larina seemed taken aback by my words, her expression softening for a moment before she quickly composed herself again. "Thank you, Your Highness. I will take that into consideration," she said, her voice low and respectful.

We spent the next few minutes sipping our tea and nibbling on the biscuits, making small talk amidst the tension that still hung in the air. Hazel kept sending me different looks as her eyes darted between me and Larina. I just shrugged like I wasn't sure what she meant, partly because I wasn't.

As we finished our tea, Larina got up to leave. I couldn't help but feel a strange sense of curiosity about her. She made her way towards the door, and I called out to her. "Larina, wait. Can we talk?" The irony of me saying those same words to Larina now didn't go unnoticed.

Larina turned, her face unreadable. "Of course, Your Highness. What can I do for you?"

I hesitated for a second; I didn't even know what I wanted to ask her or talk about. I was also unsure if I wanted to get close with another guard again after what had happened to Ben. I sighed, refusing to let this new guard see my pain. "You can just call me by my name." I decided. I still thought it was weird being called by a title—not that being called by a name other than my own was much better—but you know, it is what it is.

She nodded and bowed before leaving, still not actually addressing me by my name—or my sister's.

Thoughts of Ben and whether or not Larina would meet the same fate raced through my head as I watched her leave. I didn't want any more lives to be lost trying to save mine. My eyes watered and my throat burned as I choked back the sobs. I attempted to help matters by clearing my throat. It didn't work.

Hazel looked at me curiously, probably wondering what I was thinking. "Are you going to be okay?" she asked.

"Mmhmm." I nodded, wiping at my eyes, hoping she wouldn't see, but of course she did.

"Do you need anything?" She looked like she wanted to hug me, but I held a hand up, stopping her. It would only make me cry more.

"I'm fine. We should check on Lawrence."

She gave me a tight smile and curt nod, gesturing for me to lead the way with her outstretched arm.

We made our way to Lawrence's office, Larina walking several steps behind us, all lost in our own thoughts. I couldn't help but feel like I was being suffocated by the heaviness in the air, like the walls were closing in on me, and I struggled to keep my breathing steady.

I knocked on the door and entered. The sight of him sitting at his desk, rubbing at his temples, made my heart ache. *He must still be having nightmares about his sister*. I thought as I cleared my throat. His gaze locked on mine before darting to Hazel. He adjusted his tie and stood.

"Your Highness," he said, bowing at the waist.

"It's just us, Lawrence," I whispered, making my way to one of the empty chairs in front of his desk as Hazel clicked the door shut. Larina was stationed outside the door, waiting.

He let out a heavy sigh and practically fell back into his seat.

"Any news?" Hazel asked hopefully.

Lawrence just shook his head. "It's still early."

We knew that, but there was no harm in asking, right? Speaking of asking, I was trying to figure out just how to ask Lawrence how he was doing through all of this. Should I tell him about Amara contacting me through my dreams? Probably.

I took a deep breath, gathering my courage, before speaking. "Lawrence, I know this must be difficult for you. Is there anything we can do to help?"

He looked up at me, his eyes reflecting the exhaustion he'd been feeling. "Thank you, Avery and Hazel. Your concern means a lot," he said, his voice a little shaky.

"We're here for you," Hazel reassured him.

His eyes fell back down to his hands clasped together on his desk. "Thank you." He gave me a small smile before clearing his throat. "Speaking of being in this together, have you made any progress on finding Amara?"

"Well actually… That's part of the reason I came to see you." I mumbled barely loud enough for them to hear before basically pouring the rest out a little too quickly. "Amara has been communicating with me in some weird dream world, and she is trapped in the Shadow Lands. Wesley betrayed her, and she doesn't know how much longer she can last."

Lawrence's head shot up as he looked at me with wide eyes, taking in what I'd just said. Hazel's face was a mixture of shock and confusion, and I knew that I had just dropped a bomb on them both, especially Hazel. She knew about the powers I had and, of course, who I really was now, but I don't think I ever explained to her about the Shadow Lands themselves. I only knew what Amara had told me about them.

"What do you mean, communicating with you in a dream world?" Lawrence asked, his voice laced with disbelief.

"I don't know how to explain it exactly... It's like a different dimension, maybe? She's there, and I'm here, but we can see each other and talk to one another. It's not like a regular dream. It feels real," I explained.

Hazel leaned forward in her chair. "And she said someone betrayed her?"

"I've never met him. But she's told me about him; they were best friends."

Lawrence rubbed at his temples again. "This is a lot to take in. We need to help her, but we need to be careful."

I nodded in agreement, feeling a sense of relief that I'd told them. "I know; I just know how. She sort of explained how to get to the Shadow Lands. She told me to ask you about a safe house—that there were underground tunnels there or something."

Lawrence's expression was serious: "We'll put all our resources into finding a way to get her out. The Shadow Lands are a dangerous place, from what Amara has told me, and we don't know what we'll be up against."

"I understand," I said, my voice barely above a whisper.

Hazel reached over and took both of my hands, giving them a reassuring squeeze. "We'll figure this out together." Her eyes were filled with determination. I smiled weakly, grateful for her support in all of this, and she continued, "And who knows, maybe Xander will be back with even more guards from Coldoria to help us."

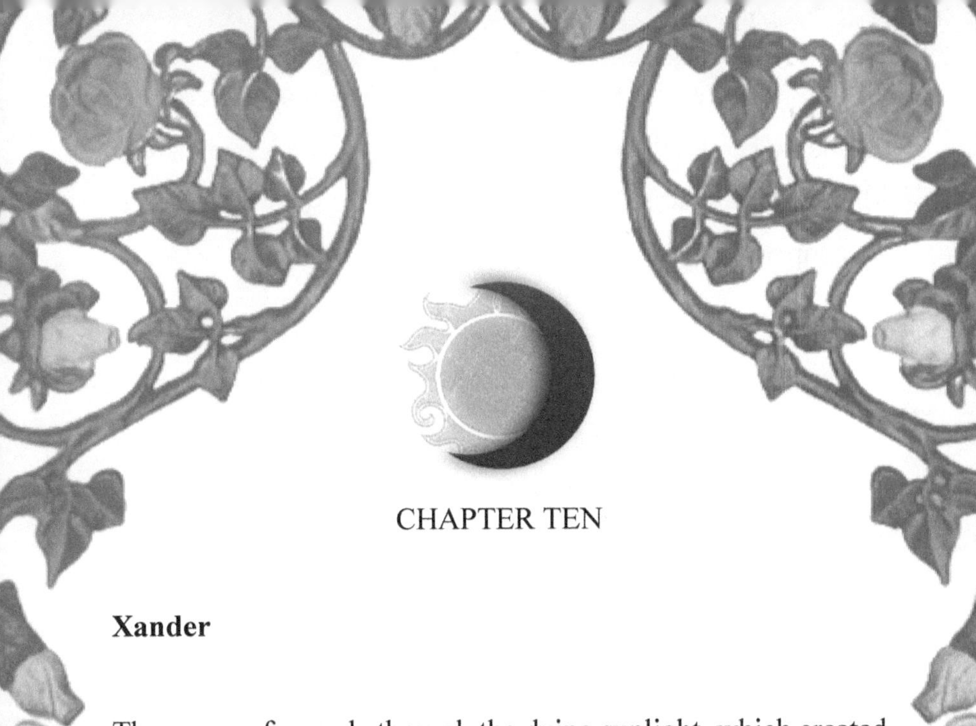

CHAPTER TEN

Xander

The group of us rode through the dying sunlight, which created a mood of unease and slowly blanketed the landscape with darkness. We could feel the temperature dropping as we neared the border between Soluna and Coldoria. The snow began to fall in thick flakes, and it was hard to make out what lay ahead—only a vast expanse of white creased with rugged terrain.

A chorus of gruff voices from the shadows broke the night's stillness as we cautiously moved forward. My initial assumption was that demons had discovered us here, but as the figures slowly emerged, I quickly realized they were people; tattered and torn rags were covering their faces. Relief washed over me that it had just been some thieves rather than something far more sinister.

My grip on the reins tightened as the bandits closed in on us. I couldn't help but wonder how many of them had been pushed to this life of crime by the harsh conditions that had befallen Coldoria. I couldn't deny that not all of the blame rested on their shoulders. My father's failed governance had sown the seeds of discontent within our kingdom.

As they encircled us, their makeshift weapons held aloft, a tense silence settled over us. Vic's hand moved subtly to the hilt of her sword, ready to spring into action at a moment's notice. Erik's steely gaze remained fixed on our assailants, his fingers twitching in anticipation.

I couldn't help but feel a twinge of guilt as I assessed the situation. These were my people, my subjects, driven to desperation by the instability of my father's rule. In some small way, their plight was a reflection of my own failures as a prince and as a leader.

But there was no time for self-pity. I needed to focus on our survival, on protecting ourselves, and the mission we were on.

"Greetings, travellers," one of the bandits spoke up, his voice gruff but polite. "We don't mean to cause any harm, but we can't let you pass through our territory without payment."

I kept my expression neutral, trying to gauge the situation. If I told them who I actually was, things could get so much worse. These bandits seemed more organized than most; perhaps there was a way to reason with them.

"We're on official business from Soluna," I said, doing my best to exude confidence without giving too much away. "We don't have any coins to spare, but perhaps we can come to a mutually beneficial agreement."

The bandit who had spoken early, seemingly the leader, raised an eyebrow and let out a low chuckle. "And what kind of agreement would that be?"

The other thieves snickered as they tightened their circle around us. Another voice among them shouted, their tone a mixture of anger and desperation. "We have nothing left to lose! Give us your valuables, and we might let you pass!"

I exchanged a knowing glance with Erik and Victoria. We were outnumbered, but we were not defenceless.

"Very well," I called out to the bandits, my voice steady. "We'll give you what we have, but I ask that you spare us unnecessary bloodshed. We are not your true enemies."

Their leader stroked his chin thoughtfully, considering my words. "Fine, we'll take what you have. And if it's not enough, we'll take your weapons and your clothes too."

Vic snorted a laugh, and I could only imagine what she thought of that comment. We couldn't afford to lose our weapons, not with the dangers lurking around from the Shadow Lands. But there was little we could do against their numbers. I nodded to Vic, silently communicating my intentions.

She dismounted from her horse and began to step forward, her sword sheathed at her side. "We'll give you *almost* everything." Her voice carried a note of authority.

The leader nodded. "We'll take what you have, and you can owe me a favour, Prince Xander."

I blinked, surprised that he had somehow recognized me. I decided to play along. "Fair enough," I said, my tone nonchalant. "But I hope we can find a way to work together in the future."

He smirked. "We'll see."

We laid down our bags, exposing the food and other supplies we'd had. The stranger eyed our offerings with a steely gaze, but to my relief—and surprise—he didn't take it all. As we rode away, I couldn't shake off the feeling that this encounter wasn't just a random one, but something more.

We moved through the snow-covered terrain without a word, our minds full of the bandits we'd just encountered. Erik had a tight grip on his reins and was as alert as ever. Victoria rode next to me, her face showing her deep thoughts, her eyes never off the land in front of us.

Our horses trotted along in unison, the sound of their hooves pounding against the earth like a soothing lullaby that begged me to get lost in my thoughts. I felt a heavy mix of guilt and determination settle into my chest as the reality of my kingdom's struggles filled my mind with worry for what lay ahead. It would only get worse if the demons decided to attack here next.

I knew that our mission to Coldoria was not just about seeking reinforcements; it was a journey to reclaim the part of their kingdom that had been lost to the shadows—and to reclaim my own kingdom from my father.

The snow-covered hills of Coldoria came into view, and I urged my horse forward. Vic and Erik followed close behind, their own horses keeping pace with mine. As we drew closer to the castle gates, my heart raced with anticipation.

Guards were stationed at the gates and waved us through after realizing who I was. Father had sent for me before, so he was probably expecting me to come; only I didn't come here because he summoned me.

We passed through an open courtyard filled with people going about their daily lives—merchants setting up stalls and children playing in the snow. Everything seemed so normal inside the castle gates, unlike the rest of the kingdom. I allowed myself a brief moment of reprieve as we dismounted from our horses in front of a large wooden door that led into the castle proper.

I took a deep breath and pushed the doors open. The familiar scent of pine and burning wood filled my nose, warming me from the cold. The castle was alive with activity; servants were cleaning and soldiers were patrolling. I nodded a greeting to the guards on duty, who gave me a respectful bow. As I made my way down the corridor, I couldn't help but feel as if I were walking into a lion's den.

Walking between the guards, they led us to the throne room. The giant wooden doors opened, and we were ushered in to find my father seated upon his golden throne. His face was stern, and his eyes narrowed as he looked at us. His court advisors surrounded him like crows around a carcass, their gazes boring into us.

"Xander," he said, his voice cold and distant.

"Father," I replied, attempting to keep my tone formal.

We stood there in silence for a moment, my father's steely gaze fixed on me. I could see the anger simmering beneath the surface, threatening to boil over at any second. I knew that I had to tread carefully.

"What brings you here?" he asked, his voice laced with contempt.

I squared my shoulders and took a step forward. "I have come on a mission to seek reinforcements from our kingdom to help Soluna. They are in dire need."

My father's lips twisted into a sarcastic smile. "And what makes you think that I would be willing to lend you aid when I have already refused?"

"What about our alliance with Soluna? Is it not our duty to send help?" I pleaded.

He let out a humourless laugh. "Our duty? Our duty is to protect our own kingdom, not to play nursemaid to those who cannot protect themselves."

I gritted my teeth, holding back my frustration. "But Soluna is a vital ally. If they fall, then our kingdom is next. We need to help them."

He leaned forward on his throne, his gaze accessing. "We need to protect our own interests. And right now, that means staying out of Soluna's problems."

My stomach sank. I knew he wouldn't help; he had already told me that when I wrote to him, but a small part of me had clung onto the hope that he might see reason. I couldn't give up. "Please, Father. You do not know what these demons are like. If we don't help Soluna, the demons will only grow stronger and come for us next."

My father leaned back on his throne, his face clouded with anger. "I have made my decision, better to let them fight it out themselves. These *demons* have no reason to attack us." He rolled his eyes as if he didn't even believe they were real. He was blind to the dangers that lurked beyond our own kingdom, and it was up to me to protect our people.

"You're wrong," I said, my chin raised in defiance.

His face twisted into a scowl; his voice full of anger. "You dare speak to me in such a manner?" He stood from his throne, his hand gripping the hilt of his sword.

The guards that had been stationed in the room all hesitated, clearly unsure of what to do. They had all witnessed this entire interaction, and I just hoped that enough of them realized how dire the situation was.

"I will not forget my duty to this kingdom. We need to act, and we need to act now."

The tension in the room was palpable as my father's court advisors shifted uneasily, their eyes darting between my father and me. I held my ground, my gaze fixed on my father, waiting for his response.

For a moment, he simply stared at me, his jaw clenched in anger. Then, suddenly, he laughed. "You are so naïve, Xander," he said, shaking his head. "You think that just because you're my son, you can come in here and tell me what to do? You're nothing but a boy playing at being a king."

"I am not a boy, Father," I said, my voice steady. "And I am not playing at being king. I am the rightful heir to this throne, and I will not stand by and watch as our kingdom falls to ruin."

My father's eyes narrowed. "You're threatening me?" he asked, his hand still gripping the hilt of his sword.

I refused to back down, determined to accomplish what I had come here for: topple my father's rule and sow seeds of unrest. There were enough guards and council members here; they would talk, and their words would spread like wildfire, burning down every last bit of support and loyalty my father thought he had.

"Not a threat, Father," I replied, taking a step closer to him. "A warning."

Suddenly, my father lunged at me with his sword, but the guards held him back. I wasn't afraid of him or the sword he wielded. I was ready to fight for what was right—to protect my kingdom from the demons and my father's tyranny.

I turned to leave, knowing that this was just the beginning of the fight that lay ahead. As I walked out of the throne room, I could feel the eyes of the guards and court advisors following me. The whispers of discontent had begun, and I hoped they would grow louder.

Walking through the castle halls, I could feel the weight of my responsibilities on my shoulders. I had to find a way to help Soluna, and I had to do it alone since my father had refused to lend aid.

But I would not let my people fall to the demons. I would rally the troops and lead them into battle. To save both Coldoria and Soluna.

CHAPTER ELEVEN

Xander

With heavy steps, I made my way to my mother's chambers. The guards outside her door bowed respectfully as I approached, allowing me to enter without question. The air inside was filled with the comforting scent of roses, a smell that had always reminded me of my mother's kindness and strength.

As I entered, she looked up from her desk, her expression as warm and welcoming as it always was. Her gentle smile instantly eased the tension in my shoulders as I crossed the room.

"Mother," I greeted, holding her tightly in my arms. "I've missed you."

Her arms wrapped around me in a loving embrace. "I've missed you too, Xander."

She stepped back with a smile, then beckoned for me to follow her over to the cluster of chairs and cushions she had arranged in the corner of the room. I sat down in one of the plush armchairs, opposite her.

"I wish I could stay longer, but there are pressing matters I must discuss with you."

Her brow furrowed. "What is it?"

I took a deep breath, steadying myself for the weight of the words I needed to speak. "Demons have been attacking Soluna, Mother. We are supposed to be their allies, yet Father is fine with letting them suffer. Not only that, but I also fear that they may turn their sights on Coldoria next."

My mother's expression shifted from concern to fear. "That is troubling news, Xander. What do you plan to do about it?"

"I plan to gather our troops and march to Soluna's aid. Our alliance with them is vital, and we cannot stand idly by as they fall."

My mother's eyes flickered with pride. "You are brave, my son. But you must be careful. Your father will not take kindly to you going against his wishes."

"I know," I said determinedly, "but I will not let his stubbornness and blindness lead our kingdom to ruin."

My mother nodded in agreement, then her eyes softened. "It's not just that, is it?"

"What do you mean?" I asked.

"You care for her now, don't you?"

"That's not important right now, Mother. What matters is that we help Soluna and protect our own kingdom."

My mother gave me a knowing smile but wisely chose not to pursue the matter further. "Very well. You have my support, Xander. As always, I will do what I can to aid you."

Relief washed over me. I knew that my mother was one of my strongest allies, and with her by my side, I felt more confident in my abilities as a leader and in getting more guards and soldiers on my side as well.

"Thank you, Mom."

She leaned closer, her voice lowering to a conspiratorial whisper. "Xander, I will do everything in my power to help you. We can gather support from the council and the court. We can show them that you are the rightful heir, the one who will lead Coldoria with wisdom and compassion." She smiled encouragingly and patted my hand. "Let's start with the court. I know they'll support you if we can prove to them that your plan is the best course of action for Coldoria."

My mother's words hung heavy in the air; her expression was serious. I knew that she was right—if I wanted to gain any support from the court and council, I would need to focus on how this plan was in Coldoria's best interest.

I nodded gratefully. "Yes, we should definitely put an emphasis on how important it is for Coldoria's future."

"So, who do you want to start with?"

I took a deep breath and thought for a moment before answering. "The Grand Duke seems like the logical choice to me. He is respected by all and holds significant authority in the court—if we can convince him of our cause, then it should go smoothly from there. I could tell from his expression during my conversation with Father that he was keenly interested in what I had to say."

She stood, nodding her agreement. "I will speak with the Grand Duke and try to sway him. You reach out to Lieutenant-General McKenna and see if he can help; he has always had a fondness for you."

Lieutenant-General Mckenna was my former teacher and had trained me when I was a boy. I felt a sense of hope and empowerment rush through me. "Thank you, Mother. I will speak with him right away."

With that, I stood up and hugged my mother tightly before heading out of her chambers to find Lieutenant-General McKenna. As I walked through the castle halls, I mentally rehearsed my speech, determined to convince him of the importance of our cause and the need for his support.

When I finally found him on the training grounds, he was sparring with some of the younger soldiers. With a smile, I approached him, watching as he easily dodged their attacks and countered with swift, precise strikes.

"Lieutenant-General McKenna," I called out, catching his attention. "May I speak with you for a moment?"

He stopped his sparring and approached me with a grin. "Prince Xander! It's been too long. What brings you here?"

I took a deep breath, steadying my nerves. "Demons have been attacking Soluna, and I plan to gather our troops and march to their aid. Our alliance with them is vital, and we cannot stand idly by as they fall."

Lieutenant-General McKenna's expression turned serious as he considered my words. "I see. And what is your father's stance on this matter?"

"He refuses to lend aid," I replied, my frustration evident.

The Lieutenant-General nodded gravely. "I understand your concern, Prince Xander. As your former teacher and someone who has watched you grow into the man you are today, I believe in your ability to lead Coldoria to greatness. I will stand with you in this fight *if* you can convince at least half of the council and my imperial guard."

I felt a surge of relief and gratitude, and a weight lifted off my shoulders. "Thank you, Lieutenant-General."

He clasped my shoulder firmly. "We will fight together, Prince Xander." He shot me a wink, as if he had no doubt in his mind that I'd be able to convince them all.

As I left the training grounds, my heart swelled with hope. With my mother and Lieutenant-General McKenna on my side, I knew it was possible. McKenna was never fond of my father, but he could never do anything against him until now. He knew the horrible things my father had done to this kingdom and to me. It was part of the reason he had trained so early on.

As I made my way back to my chambers, I couldn't help but think about how far we had come. From being a young boy and watching my father's cruelty and coldness to now standing up against him for the sake of our people. It was a daunting task, but I was ready for it.

When I reached my chambers, I sat down and started drafting a plan. I knew that I would need to approach the council with a solid argument, one that would convince them that aiding Soluna was in Coldoria's best interest. I needed to make them see that our alliance with Soluna was vital and that turning our backs on them would only lead to consequences. I needed them to understand that we had to take a stand for what was right, even if it meant going against my father.

My head jerked up, and I gasped at the sound of a loud, insistent knock on the door. I was slumped over my desk, surrounded by papers, and must have dozed off at some point last night while planning for today. With a groan, I rubbed my eyes and made my way towards the door.

It was my mother. She wore a serious expression on her face, and I held the door open for her to come in.

"The council will be meeting as the Grand Duke has requested it. They, together with a large number of imperial guards, have assembled here to listen to your case."

My heart skipped a beat at my mother's words. This was it. The moment I had been preparing for. I took a deep breath, trying to steady my nerves.

"Thank you, Mother. Let's go."

We made our way to the council chamber, where the Grand Duke and the other council members were waiting for us. I could feel their eyes on me as I walked in, their faces grave and serious.

"Prince Xander," the Grand Duke said, nodding to me. "We have heard of your plan to aid Soluna in their time of need. Please explain to us why you believe this is in Coldoria's best interest."

I stood tall, trying to exude confidence. "Soluna is our ally. Their fall would not only be a loss for them but also for us. We must stand together in times of crisis. Furthermore, the demons attacking Soluna may turn their sights on Coldoria next. We cannot afford to wait and see what happens. We must act now to protect our people and our kingdom."

The council members murmured amongst themselves, but the Grand Duke raised his hand in silence. "And what does your father, King Alexander, have to say about this matter?"

I hesitated; we both knew that my father's refusal to aid Soluna was a sore spot for many in the council, but I also knew that I needed to be honest. "My father does not support this plan, but I believe it is the right course of action for Coldoria."

The Grand Duke stroked his beard thoughtfully. "Very well. We will take your proposal into consideration and make a decision at a later time."

I could feel my heart sinking. This wasn't the resounding support I had hoped for, but I knew it was a start. Before I could say anything, my mother stepped forward, her voice firm and unwavering.

"Excuse me, Grand Duke, but I believe that Prince Xander has presented a compelling argument for why we must aid Soluna. As the Queen of Coldoria, I stand with my son in his plan to gather our troops and march to their aid. I urge all of you to consider the greater good of our kingdom and support Prince Xander in his efforts to protect our people."

I felt a surge of pride and gratitude for my mother as she spoke, her words echoing in the chamber. The other council members appeared to be moved by her conviction as well, and I could see them nodding in agreement.

The Grand Duke looked thoughtful for a moment before finally speaking. "Very well, Queen Desiree. We will take your words into consideration as well. We will reconvene in two days to make our decision."

Just as everyone moved to leave, my father entered the council room. His eyes narrowed as he took in the scene before him, his gaze lingering on me and my mother. "What is the meaning of this?" he demanded.

"We were discussing Prince Xander's proposal to aid Soluna," the Grand Duke replied calmly.

My father scoffed. "Ridiculous. We have enough problems of our own to deal with. We cannot waste our resources on a foolish venture."

I felt my blood boil at his dismissive words, but before I could say anything, my mother stepped forward.

"King Alexander, I must respectfully disagree. Our alliance with Soluna is important to our kingdom, and we must stand by them in their time of need. I believe Prince Xander's plan is the right course of action." Her words were measured but firm.

My father's eyes darted between my mother and me, his expression growing darker with each passing moment. "You would both betray me and our kingdom? This is treason."

The council members shifted uncomfortably at the accusation, but my mother stood her ground. "We are not betraying anyone, Alexander. We are doing what is best for Coldoria."

My father's face twisted in rage as he took a menacing step forward. "You would dare to defy me? I am the King of Coldoria!"

My mother and I exchanged a worried glance as my father continued to rage, his words growing more and more irrational. It was clear that he would not be swayed by reason and that we were in danger.

As my father raised his hand to strike my mother, I knew that I had to act. I lunged forward, pushing her out of the way and taking the blow myself. The force of the hit knocked me to the ground, and I could feel blood trickling down the side of my face.

My father looked shocked for a moment before turning on his heel and storming out of the council chamber, leaving behind a tense silence.

But I knew that my mother and Lieutenant-General McKenna's support gave me the foundation I needed to continue pushing for our plan to aid Soluna. And with the council reconvening in two days, I had a newfound hope that we could convince them to stand with us as well.

CHAPTER TWELVE

Amara

My laughter echoed through the royal stables as I watched Wesley try to mount a spirited black steed. The sun dipped low on the horizon, casting a warm glow over the kingdom, and the air was filled with the sounds of neighing horses and the rustle of straw.

"Come on, Wes! You have to swing your leg over more gracefully," I teased, my eyes sparkling with mischief.

Wesley, red-faced but determined, tried again. This time, with a bit more finesse, he managed to straddle the horse.

"I think I'm getting the hang of it," Wesley said, his eyes bright.

I nodded approvingly. "Now, hold onto the reins and give him a gentle pat on the neck. Let him know you're in charge."

As he followed my instructions, I walked over to my own horse, a beautiful chestnut mare named Abi. I patted Abi's flank affectionately, sharing a quiet moment with her.

"You don't have to do this, you know," Wesley said as he cautiously guided the horse forward.

I turned to him, my expression serious. "I want to. It was part of our deal, and I need to know how to protect myself; besides, it's more fun if we can ride together."

Wesley's gaze softened. "You're the most unconventional princess I know."

"And just how many other princesses do you know?" I chuckled, teasing him again.

Wesley grinned. "Just you, Amara. But that's enough for me."

I felt a warmth spread through me at his words, but I quickly pushed it aside. I couldn't let myself get distracted by thoughts of him.

We rode out of the stables and onto the dirt path that led towards the forest. The breeze was cool against my face, and I felt free and unburdened. For a moment, I forgot about the responsibilities that came with being a princess and just enjoyed the simple pleasure of riding. This was one of the things I loved most about spending time with Wesley; he always made me feel free.

We left the stables, and my mount trotted ahead, quickly gaining momentum as we rode out onto the dirt path that snaked through the woods. I felt the wind whip against my face as we galloped further away, making me feel relieved and liberated in a way I hadn't been for a while.

The trees grew thicker with each passing hour, blocking out most of the sun's rays before they finally disappeared beneath the horizon. We were soon relying on the moonlight streaming through the canopy to light our way. All we could hear was the steady thud of horses' hooves hitting the ground, and it seemed to soothe me, like an old lullaby that brought me peace and comfort.

We rode on for what felt like hours, the darkness of the forest surrounding us like a warm embrace. Wesley and I were in perfect sync as we navigated the winding path, our horses moving effortlessly together.

As we finally emerged from the woods, a clearing came into view, and my heart lifted at the sight. The moon was high in the sky, casting a silver light over the small lake that lay before us. It was one of my favourite spots in the kingdom, a peaceful oasis that always brought me a sense of calm.

Without a word, Wesley and I dismounted and led our horses to the edge of the lake. We sat down on the soft grass, our backs against a tree, and gazed out at the serene water.

For a few moments, we sat in silence, content to simply be in each other's company. But then Wesley turned to me, his eyes intense.

"Amara," he said, his voice low.

"Yes," I replied, turning to face him. Our faces were so close where we sat that I could feel the warmth of his breath as he spoke.

His eyes shifted for a moment, and then he cleared his throat and turned to face the water once more.

"You're going to be queen one day," he said finally, though a part of me thought he might have wanted to say something else, like he was holding something back.

"Not if I can help it," I admitted. "I'd rather face a dragon than sit on the throne."

He rolled his eyes while chuckling to himself. "Well, you'd be the most fearsome queen the kingdom has ever seen."

I nudged him with my elbow. "Stop it. I'm serious. I just want a simple life, Wesley. No crowns, no royal duties."

He turned to me again, a twinkle in his eyes. "What if you find someone who makes the royal life worth it?"

My cheeks warmed, and I hesitated for a moment, unsure of how to respond. I looked away, unable to meet his gaze. "Nonsense. That someone doesn't exist."

"We'll see," he said, and I couldn't help but notice the grin that spread across his face from the corner of my eye.

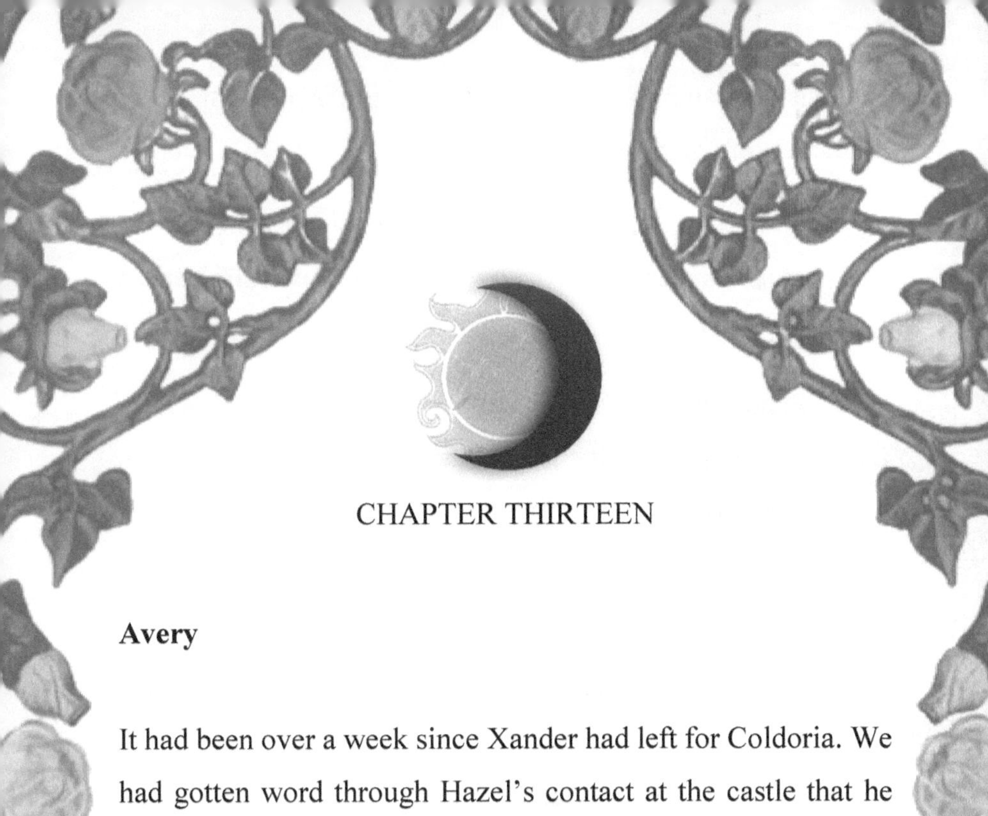

CHAPTER THIRTEEN

Avery

It had been over a week since Xander had left for Coldoria. We had gotten word through Hazel's contact at the castle that he had arrived, but that was all we had heard. We weren't sure how his plan was going or if he was even okay.

I couldn't help but worry, pacing back and forth in our small hideout. Hazel was sitting at the table, staring at a map of Coldoria, her brow furrowed in concentration. She looked up at me as I passed by for the tenth time and sighed.

"Avery, you need to calm down. Xander is a capable prince; he can handle himself."

"I know, but it's been so long since we've heard anything. What if something happens to him?" My voice wavered.

Hazel stood up and placed a comforting hand on my shoulder. "We can only hope and pray that he's safe. But we can't sit here and do nothing. We need to keep planning and preparing for when he returns."

She was right. We couldn't let our worry consume us. We had to trust Xander and focus on what was happening here in Soluna.

It had been oddly peaceful and free of any more attacks from Esmeray. I wasn't sure if she was just planning something even more sinister or if she was trying to lull us into a false sense of security before striking.

Either way, we were still taking no chances. Chaz was back in the dungeons, although I wasn't sure how he kept escaping them. Then again, I also wasn't sure how he was even alive. I suspected that Esmeray had her hand in that as well, which meant we needed to be on high alert.

Hazel and I moved quickly through the streets of Soluna, our minds spinning with plans for supplies. The townspeople were starting to become wary, their nerves frayed from the constant threat of Esmeray's forces looming over them. We had to act fast if we wanted to prepare for anything that might come our way.

We went from merchant to merchant, gathering what we needed to keep our forces prepared for any potential attack. We stockpiled food, medical supplies, weaponry, and anything else that could be useful in a battle.

It was hard work, but it gave me something productive to focus on while we waited to hear from Xander's mission. Not knowing how things were going in Coldoria only added to my anxiety as the days passed by without any news of his return.

No matter what I did, I felt like it wasn't enough for anyone. I hadn't heard anything else from Amara, and I was worried that it would take too long to get to the Shadow Lands to rescue her. My stomach twisted with dread at the thought of marching down there without a real plan. I knew that we couldn't just sit around and wait for things to happen. We had to take action.

Hazel and I spent our time helping around Soluna however we could. In the evenings, Hazel would go to the infirmary. She bustled around, handing Midge medicine and water, changing bandages, and calming agitated patients with her gentle touch.

Meanwhile, I was in the stables training, trying to hone my powers and create new abilities that could be useful in a fight against Esmeray's forces. I was determined to turn water droplets into spikes of ice that I could use as weapons against our enemies.

Narrowing my focus and intense concentration, I closed my eyes, visualizing the water droplets in front of me. Carefully, I channelled my energy and, with a wave of my hands, turned them into sharp icicles. I opened my eyes and watched as they carved through the air like miniature spears. With a sense of accomplishment, I smiled to myself, knowing that this would be incredibly useful during another attack.

My shoulders slumped then; I hadn't been able to create my water nymphs again since the last attack on Estrella. But I couldn't dwell on my failures. I needed to keep practicing, keep training, and keep preparing for whatever was to come. We needed to be ready for whatever awaited us when Xander returned with news from Coldoria—or if he didn't come back at all.

Hazel stepped into the barn, and I watched from the corner of my eye while she sat down on a stack of hay next to Larina. The two of them talked, laughing at something that must have been funny. I couldn't help but smile as I saw how content Hazel was in her own skin. Despite all the darkness looming over us, she managed to find joy in the simplest things. It was inspiring.

But our moment of peace was short-lived. The sound of footsteps echoed through the barn, alerting us to an intruder. We turned to face the door, ready to defend ourselves if needed.

But it wasn't an enemy that entered the barn; it was Xander.

My heart leapt with relief at the sight of him, but my joy was short-lived as I saw the exhaustion etched on his face. He looked like he hadn't slept in days, and his clothes were torn and stained with blood. My worry for him returned in full force.

"Hazel, Amara," Xander said, his voice hoarse. His eyes shifted towards Larina and then back to me. "We need to talk."

I nodded. "Larina, keep watch."

She bowed, then made her way to the entrance to stand guard. Hazel and I followed Xander to the far side of the barn. Xander took a deep breath and started to speak.

"Coldoria is in chaos. My father has lost his grip on reality and is lashing out at everyone around him. The council has sided with me and agreed to send forces to help. But now my father has accused us of treason and tried to have me arrested. I barely managed to escape, but I don't know how long I can stay safe. We need to act fast before he does something drastic."

My heart sank at the news. It seemed like every day brought more bad news and more danger. But we couldn't give up now. We had come too far and sacrificed too much to let everything fall apart.

"How did you manage to escape?" Hazel asked, placing a comforting hand on his arm, and he gave her a sad smile before continuing.

"We had to fight our way out of the castle and flee through the mountains to get here."

Hazel's eyes widened. "How many soldiers did you have with you?"

"Enough; we were lucky not to have too many casualties. But we lost some good men and women," Xander replied, his eyes flickering with grief.

I could see the pain in his eyes as he spoke. He was carrying the weight of everything that had happened on his shoulders, and it was taking its toll on him.

"We need to plan our next move. If we don't, my father will continue to escalate the situation until it reaches a point of no return," Xander said, his voice steady despite his weariness. "The Lord Regent has already escorted my soldiers to a place where they can rest for the night."

Hazel and I nodded, determined to help in any way we could. We knew that this was our fight too, and we weren't going to give up until we had won.

"We'll start planning tomorrow. For now, you need rest," I said, placing my hand on Xander's shoulder. "We're glad you're back, and we'll do everything we can to help."

Xander smiled weakly, and I could see the gratitude in his eyes. He was glad to be back, but he also knew that the fight was far from over. We all did. We were in this together, and we would do whatever it took to protect our people and bring peace back to Soluna and Coldoria.

I asked Larina to escort Hazel back to her quarters, and Xander walked me back to mine. As we walked through the dark corridors, I could feel a heavy weight pressing down on my chest. Xander seemed just as exhausted, but he was determined not to show it. We both knew what we had to do, and we were ready to face whatever challenges lay ahead of us.

When we arrived at my room, Xander gave me a tired smile. "I'm glad you're still here with me. I wouldn't have made it through this without you."

My heart swelled with affection for him. Even in the face of overwhelming difficulties, he remained courageous and strong. "I'll always be here for you, Xander. No matter what happens, we'll face it together."

We stood there in the dim light of the hallway, just looking into each other's eyes. I could feel the electricity sparking between us—the unspoken connection that had been growing stronger. I wanted nothing more than to kiss him, to hold him close, and to forget about all the troubles in the world.

But before I could act on my impulse, Xander took a step back, breaking the spell. "Get some rest, Avery," he said, his voice quiet but firm. "We have a lot of work to do tomorrow."

Nodding, I felt a mixture of disappointment and understanding. He was right; we had to stay focused and keep our priorities straight. "Sleep well, Xander," I said softly as I watched him walk away.

As I closed the door to my room, I couldn't help but feel a sense of longing. I wanted to be close to him, to share his burdens and his triumphs. But I also knew that our fight wasn't over yet and that we couldn't afford to let our emotions get in the way.

I changed into my night clothes and climbed into bed, my mind racing with thoughts of what was to come. As I drifted off to sleep, I knew that I would need all my strength and determination to face the challenges ahead—but then reality set in once more and reminded me that no matter how hard we tried, there was always something lurking beneath the surface, threatening to tear us apart again.

I let out a deep, heavy sob as tears began to pour down my face, soaking the pillow beneath me. In a desperate attempt to run away from my sorrows, I yanked the covers up over my head, smothering myself in darkness and hoping for a sweet and numb escape in sleep.

CHAPTER FOURTEEN

Avery

When I woke up the next morning, I felt the heaviness of the previous night's events weighing down on me. But I also felt a sense of determination. We had to keep fighting, no matter what. Soluna and Coldoria depended on us.

I got out of bed and began to get dressed, ready to face the day ahead. As I put on my clothes, I couldn't help but think about Xander. I missed him, and I wanted to see him again. I knew we had to focus on the mission, but I couldn't ignore my feelings either.

When I stepped out of my room, I saw Xander waiting for me in the hallway. He had a serious expression on his face, but his eyes lit up when he saw me.

"Good morning, Avery," he said, his voice low and smooth.

"Good morning, Xander," I replied, trying to keep my voice neutral.

"We need to start planning our next move," Xander said, his tone grave. "But first, I need to talk to you alone."

My heart skipped a beat as he took my hand and led me to a quiet corner of the hallway. I wondered what he wanted to talk to me about, but I could feel the intensity of his gaze on me, making me feel both nervous and excited.

"Avery," he began, taking a deep breath. "I don't know how to say this, but...I can't stop thinking about you."

My heart raced as I searched his face for any sign of hesitation or doubt. But all I saw was raw emotion and vulnerability.

"Xander..." I started, but he cut me off.

"I know we have a lot on our plates right now. But I can't help how I feel. I need to know if you feel the same way," he said, his eyes never leaving mine.

I took a deep breath, feeling a mix of fear and excitement. This was what I had wanted, but I hadn't expected it to happen now, in the midst of all the chaos.

"I do feel the same way, Xander," I said, my voice barely above a whisper.

Relief washed over his face, and he pulled me into a tight embrace. I wrapped my arms around him, feeling safe and loved.

"You don't know how much this means to me, Avery," he said, his voice shaking with emotion.

I pulled away slightly, looking up at him. "We have to be careful, Xander. We can't let our feelings get in the way of our mission."

He nodded. "You're right. We should start planning," Xander said, his tone serious once again. "But I want you to know that I'm here for you, Avery. Always."

We stood there for a moment longer, just looking at each other, before Xander leaned in and kissed me. It was a soft, gentle kiss, but it held so much emotion and longing. I thought back to the night before he left for Coldoria and hoped he wouldn't have to leave me like that again.

As we pulled away from each other, Xander's eyes were filled with both desire and determination. "We'll get through this together, Avery. I promise."

I nodded, feeling a sense of relief wash over me. I had never felt so connected to anyone before, and I knew that no matter what challenges we faced, we would face them together.

As we began to walk towards the planning room, I couldn't ignore the butterflies in my stomach. I was scared of what was to come, but I was also excited to see where this newfound connection with Xander would take us.

Xander stepped aside and held the door open for me as I entered. The room was cramped with a large hardwood table in its centre, taking up the majority of the space. Everyone was already seated around the table; the air was thick with anticipation.

Lawrence was seated at the end of one of the sides of the table, leaving the head of the table spot open for me. I sat down, with Xander taking the empty seat next to me and opposite Lawrence.

Hazel, Erik, Victoria, and Larina were the only other familiar faces in the room. The others were a mix of people wearing Solunian royal guard uniforms and Coldoria's burgundy and black.

Lawrence cleared his throat, bringing my attention back to him. "Good morning, everyone. As you all know, we have a very important task ahead of us. We need to get to the Shadow Lands for a rescue mission and defeat the Shadow Lord."

There were murmurs of agreement around the table, but I could sense the tension in the room. We couldn't exactly tell them *who* we were rescuing.

Xander cleared his throat, and the whispers instantly stopped, all eyes on him as he spoke. "The council has sent word. They will be sending more reinforcements from Coldoria.

We didn't want to risk bringing everyone. We didn't want to attract too much attention, and it's easier to move around with a smaller group. We'll need to coordinate with them once they arrive."

There were nods of understanding from the group, and I could sense the collective resolve.

"But first, we need to make a plan of attack," Xander continued. "We have some intel on the Shadow Lord's stronghold, but we'll need to gather more information before we can proceed. Hazel, Erik, and Victoria will be in charge of reconnaissance. We need to know the location of the prisoners, the number of guards, and any possible escape routes.

Getting in will be the easy part; it's getting out that will be the real struggle. There is a magical barrier that is keeping everyone inside. Lawrence and Larina will be in charge of creating distractions to draw Shadow Lord out so we can defeat her and bring down the barrier."

I sat silently, listening as Xander assigned the rest of the tasks. I couldn't help but feel a sense of gratitude towards Xander for being such a good leader. Bringing down the barrier would be on me and Amara, but I knew together we could do it.

After the meeting, Xander and I retreated to the stables so we could train some more. We needed to discuss our plan of action, but before we could do that, Xander pinned me against the wall and kissed me passionately.

I melted into his embrace, feeling my pulse race and my body heat up. But as much as I wanted to lose myself in the moment and forget about everything else, I knew we had to focus.

"Xander," I said, breaking away from the kiss. "We need to talk about the plan."

He sighed, his forehead resting on mine. "I know. I just can't help myself when I'm near you, love." Xander pulled away reluctantly and took a few steps back. He ran a hand through his hair and looked away.

I smiled softly at him, and he finally met my gaze before smiling back.

"You're right," he said gruffly.

I nodded and cleared my throat before beginning. "The first thing we have to do is find out where the Shadow Lord is keeping the prisoners. I know they're in some sort of dungeon, but that's all I know. I haven't been able to contact Amara in that dream world since before you left for Coldoria."

Xander nodded thoughtfully. "I'll talk to Hazel, Erik, and Victoria tonight and see if we can come up with a plan to get the information we need. They'll bring a falcon with them, and we just have to hope it'll be able to get through the barrier with their letters. We also need to start thinking about how we're going to bring down that magical barrier once we have the location of Amara and the others."

"What if I could get my water nymphs inside the barrier and figure out where Amara is? They won't be as easily detected by Esmeray, and I can have contact with them the entire time. We wouldn't have to risk sending anyone inside the barrier until we know where they're being kept."

Xander's eyes widened in surprise. "That's brilliant, Avery. But how would you communicate with them if they're inside the barrier?"

"I have a magical connection with my water nymphs. I can talk to them telepathically. And they can communicate with each other as well," I explained, not mentioning the fact that I hadn't been able to summon them since the last attack, but I would figure it out. I had to.

Xander nodded, impressed. "Alright, we'll go with that plan. But we still need to figure out how to bring down the barrier once we have the location of the prisoners. Do you have any ideas?"

I bit my lip in thought. "I might have a solution, but it's risky," I said hesitantly.

Xander raised an eyebrow. "I'm listening."

"I could try to tap into the dark magic that Esmeray is using to power the barrier. If I can figure out how it works, I might be able to neutralize it or even reverse it," I explained.

Xander looked skeptical. "Avery, dark magic is extremely dangerous. You could get hurt, or worse."

"I know it's dangerous," I said firmly. "But we don't have any other options right now. Me and Amara's combined magic might be strong enough to bring it down. But it might not. And we don't know if she'll be in any state to help us. We have to get our people out of there. And if there's even a chance that I can save them, I have to take it."

Xander looked at me, his expression conflicted. "I don't like it, but I understand. Just promise me that you'll be careful."

"I will," I promised.

As we continued to discuss the plan, I couldn't help but feel grateful for Xander's support and faith in me. Together, we would face any challenge that came our way. And no matter what happened, I hoped we wouldn't have to leave each other like we did before.

But I pushed those thoughts aside and focused on the task ahead. We had a plan, and we would see it through. We spent the rest of the day training and preparing for what lay ahead. Now, I *needed* to be able to call on my water nymphs again.

I tried for hours with no results. As the sun began to set, I left Xander to go down to the pond. After checking that I was truly alone, I stood by the edge of the water, closed my eyes, and took a deep breath. I reached out with my magic, searching for any sign of my water nymphs. But as I stretched out my senses, I felt nothing but a cold emptiness. My heart sank. *What had happened? Why can't I summon them like before?*

I tried again, concentrating harder this time. But still, there was nothing. Not even a flicker of energy. What was going on?

Desperate for answers, I plunged my hand into the water. Begging the well of magic inside of me to do something, *anything.*

I was about to give up when I felt a cold breeze brush against my skin. I opened my eyes and saw a figure hovering above the water in the middle of the pond. *Calypso.*

"Avery," Calypso's soft voice whispered. "I'm sorry I haven't been able to answer your call. Esmeray has grown stronger. And her power has weakened our connection. But I have something important to tell you."

My heart leapt. Not only had I finally made contact with Calypso again, but for once, she wasn't being cryptic. 'What is it? Where are Amara and the others?"

Calypso hesitated before speaking. "Amara is not with the others. Esmeray has kept her in a separate chamber, and she's been using her as a source of power to enhance her magic."

I gasped, horrified. "Is she okay? Can she fight?"

"She's alive, but weak," Calypso said. "And I fear she won't be able to help you bring down the barrier. But there is something else you can do."

"What?" I asked, practically shouting at her in desperation.

Her words were muffled as if they had been sealed in a silent vacuum, yet her mouth kept moving. Knowing I had to get closer, I sprinted, plunging into the water that seemed to be slowly stealing her away from me. My heart was pounding quicker with each passing second, and I stretched out my hand for her but only felt the emptiness of air as she became a distant memory.

CHAPTER FIFTEEN

Avery

I burst out of the pond, gasping for air. Tears streamed down my face as I tried to process what Calypso had just told me. Amara was alive, but barely. And she was being used to enhance Esmeray's magic. I couldn't let this continue.

I raced back up to the training grounds, where Xander was waiting for me. He looked up at me, concern etched on his face. "Avery, what's wrong?"

I took a deep breath, trying to steady my voice. "I finally made contact with Calypso. Amara is alive, but she's being used to enhance Esmeray's magic. We have to do something, Xander."

He nodded, his eyes steely with determination. "We will. But first, we need to focus on getting the information we need about where the prisoners are being held. Did you have any luck with your water nymphs?"

I shook my head, feeling defeated. "No, I still can't summon them. But I have a feeling that it has something to do with Esmeray's magic as well. I need to figure out how to counteract it."

Xander put a hand on my shoulder. "Don't worry, we'll figure it out together. For now, let's focus on getting our people out of there. We'll deal with Esmeray and her magic later."

I nodded, feeling a sense of determination wash over me. We had a plan, and we would see it through no matter what.

The next few days were spent preparing for the mission. Xander and I worked on perfecting our battle strategies, and I tried to find a way to counteract Esmeray's magic. It was a difficult task, but I refused to give up. I knew that we had to save Amara and the others, and I would do whatever it took to make that happen.

There was one more thing I needed to do before we were ready to leave for the Shadow Lands. I needed to go visit my mom in the mortal world, just in case.

I knew how dangerous this mission was going to be, and I wanted to make sure that I didn't regret not seeing my mom one last time if things didn't go as planned. Xander understood and agreed to come with me for support.

Lawrence had prepared the carriage that would transport us to the mortal world.

As we rode in the carriage, I couldn't help but feel nervous. The last time I had seen my mom, I had left so abruptly that I hadn't been able to properly say goodbye. And now, I was about to go on a dangerous mission, one that could potentially end in my death. The thought of not being able to see her again made my heart ache.

As if sensing my unease, Xander took my hand in his and squeezed it gently.

"It's going to be okay, Avery. We'll make it back in one piece, I promise," he said, his voice soft and reassuring.

I looked at him, feeling a sense of gratitude wash over me. "Thank you, Xander. I don't know what I'd do without you."

He smiled at me. "You don't have to worry about that. I'll always be by your side."

With his words echoing in my mind, we arrived at my mom's house. I took a deep breath, steadying myself before getting out of the carriage, which, of course, had turned into the impala on the outside.

Xander followed close behind me, his presence a source of comfort. My heart pounded in my chest as I walked up to the door and knocked. My mom answered almost immediately, looking surprised to see me.

"Avery! What are you doing here?" She asked, her eyes scanning me up and down as if trying to see if anything was wrong.

"I just wanted to come say hi, Mom. And let you know that I love you," I said, feeling my eyes start to fill with tears despite my best efforts to hold them back.

My mom's face softened, and she pulled me into a hug. "I love you too, sweetie. Is everything okay?"

I hesitated for a moment, wondering if I should tell her about the dangerous mission we were about to embark on. But I knew that she deserved to know the truth.

"Mom, I'm going on a mission to save some friends. It's dangerous, and I don't know what's going to happen," I said, my voice cracking with emotion.

My mom pulled away from the hug, her eyes widening in concern. "What kind of mission? Is there anything I can do to help?"

Xander stepped forward, his posture confident and reassuring. "We're going to a place known as the Shadow Lands to rescue some prisoners. It's dangerous, but we've been training for it. We just wanted to come say goodbye before we left.”

My mom nodded, her eyes misting with tears. "Please be careful. And come back to me in one piece.”

I hugged her tightly, my heart heavy with emotion. “I will, Mom. I promise.”

“How long can you stay here?” she asked.

I looked to Xander, and he took this as his que to give us some time alone. “I’ll just be outside,” he said before stepping out.

My mom and I sat down on the couch, and I told her everything that had happened since I left for Soluna. I told her about my magic, my friends, and my long-lost sister, whom she apparently already knew about, and the danger we were facing. She listened intently, asking questions and offering words of encouragement.

“I’m so proud of you, Avery,” she said, her hand on mine. “I always knew you were meant for something great.”

Her words brought tears to my eyes, and I hugged her again. “Thank you, Mom.”

We talked for a little while longer, catching up on everything that had happened while I was away.

Xander came back in, informing us that it was time to go.

She nodded, wiping away tears from her eyes. "I understand. I'm just glad I got to see you before you left."

"I'm glad too," I said, my voice cracking with emotion.

We hugged again before I finally had to tear myself away and head back out to the magical car.

"Are you okay?" he asked, his voice gentle as he helped me into the car.

I nodded, trying to hold back my tears. "Yeah, let's just go."

"We'll make it back, Avery. And we'll get Amara and the others out," he said as he sat down next to me in the back seat.

Finally, the day of the mission arrived. Erik and Victoria had gone to the safe house Amara had told me about to see if they could find anything useful.

The plan was for a small group of us to go back to the Safe House and use the underground tunnels to get to the Shadow Lands, while the rest marched south until they reached where the barrier should be.

Our small group would consist of Xander, myself, Erik, Victoria, Hazel, and Larina. Lawrence remained at the castle to keep an eye on things here. Xander's former instructor would be leading the large group to the borders.

I tapped my foot impatiently, waiting for everyone to gather at the castle gates. Everyone was there, with the exception of Erik and Victoria. When they still hadn't arrived ten minutes later, Xander and I exchanged worried glances.

"Where are they?" I asked, my voice barely more than a whisper.

"I don't know," Xander said, looking at me in concern. "But we can't wait any longer. We need to go."

I nodded and gathered my things. I could tell that he was worried, but he didn't show it. Instead, he put on a brave face and reassured me that everything would be okay. I swallowed my fears and followed him through the gates.

As we walked down the dirt road, I couldn't help but start to have doubts about my plan. What if I couldn't counter Esmeray's magic? Was Amara okay? Was she in pain? Or what if we couldn't get her out in time? I tried to push those thoughts aside, focusing on the task at hand. We had to stay strong and keep moving forward.

The journey was long and grueling. We walked for hours on end, the sun beating down on us mercilessly. The closer we got to the Shadow Lands, the more I felt the weight of our mission bearing down on me. But I refused to let it break me. We had come too far to give up now.

As we approached the safe house, we saw Erik and Victoria waiting for us outside. They looked relieved to see us, and I could tell that they had found something important.

"Did you find anything useful?" I asked as we approached them.

"Yes," Erik said, nodding. "We found a map of the Shadow Lands. It should help us navigate through the tunnels."

I breathed a sigh of relief. "Thank you, Erik. That's a huge help." I wasn't sure exactly how he had gotten a hold of this map; I just hoped it wasn't a trap set here by Esmeray and her demons.

We made our way inside the safe house, checking the tunnels for any signs of danger. It was quiet, the only sound being the clicking of our boots against the stone floor. I couldn't shake the feeling that we were being watched, but I brushed it off as paranoia.

As I stepped cautiously into the large opening, my eyes widened in amazement. I had never seen anything like it. The walls of the cavern were lined with intricate carvings of the sun and moon. They glowed with a faint silver light that illuminated the entire room.

I glanced around nervously, expecting an attack at any moment. But there was nothing but silence. For a moment, I let my guard down, taking in the beauty of this place. It was breathtakingly beautiful, and something about it made me feel at peace.

But then reality set in, and I remembered why we were here: to rescue Amara from Esmeray's clutches. I steeled myself for what was to come and stepped forward into the unknown. We left the glowing tavern behind and continued down the dark pathways of the tunnels.

Xander followed close behind me, one hand resting on my shoulder in silent support as we moved deeper into the passage. We reached a fork in the road, leading us left or right. We both hesitated for a moment before agreeing to take the left path.

It seemed quieter than the right one, and so we ventured off in that direction. The further we went, the darker it became, until finally all light disappeared completely from view, save for the flickering of our own torches.

I couldn't help but feel a sense of foreboding as we continued down the tunnel. It was as if the darkness was pressing in on us, suffocating us with its weight. I could hear the sound of my heart beating in my ears, and I wondered if the others could hear it too.

Suddenly, we heard whispers up ahead. We exchanged a quick glance of concern before picking up our pace, our weapons at the ready.

We rounded a corner, and my heart skipped a beat at the sight before us. A group of demons were waiting for us.

Their red eyes glowed in the darkness, and their sharp teeth glinted in the dim light of our torches. I could feel the fear creeping up inside me, threatening to overwhelm me completely.

But I knew that I couldn't let that happen. I had to stay strong, for Amara and for everyone else who was counting on us.

Xander stepped in front of me. "Let me handle this," he said, his voice steady.

He unsheathed his sword and charged toward the demons. They met him with equal ferocity, but Xander was a skilled warrior. He dodged and weaved, his sword slicing through the air as he struck blow after blow against the demons.

Erik dashed into the chaos, his sword slicing through demons with ease. Victoria and Larina followed close behind, their swords whirling around them in a dizzying blur of motion.

I took a deep breath and closed my eyes, focusing on the rushing currents of the water inside me. I could feel them shifting, gathering like a storm before releasing in a flood of power.

Opening my eyes, I sent a fierce blast of water towards the demons. As the force of my attack knocked them back, they hissed and shrieked. Xander and the others took advantage of their momentary weakness, raining down blows upon them. Their glowing eyes widened as they struggled to get back up, but I was ready.

With another surge of power, I called forth a raging torrent of water that seemed almost luminescent. It surged towards the demons, sweeping them off their feet and slamming them against the walls of the tunnel. I could hear their screams echoing through the darkness before they burst into smoke and ash, then vanished completely.

Breathless, I turned to see Xander and the others staring at me in awe.

"You did it," Xander said, a grin spreading across his face.

I smiled back, feeling a sense of satisfaction wash over me. We had made it through the first obstacle, and we were one step closer to rescuing Amara.

We continued down the tunnel, encountering more demons along the way. But with each battle, we grew stronger and more confident in our abilities to defeat them.

Eventually, we came to what seemed like a dead end. "This must be it," I called out to the others while I felt around for the tiny opening Amara had said they'd slipped through.

After a few moments of searching, I found the small crevice in the wall. It was just big enough for us to squeeze through, but it was dark on the other side. I hesitated; we would have to leave our torches behind to fit, and I wondered if we were making the right decision. But I thought of Amara, alone and suffering, and I knew that we had to keep going.

I held my breath as I squeezed through the tiny opening, feeling the cold stone walls against my skin. Xander followed close behind, his shoulder digging into mine. The darkness seemed to swallow us up as we sidestepped through in single file.

Light finally broke through, and I made my way towards it. As we emerged from the narrow passageway, my eyes widened at the sight before us. We were in a forest full of pink cherry blossoms.

The trees towered above us, their boughs heavy with delicate petals. Shafts of sunlight filtered through the leaves, casting a soft glow on the forest floor. It was a stark contrast to the dark and foreboding tunnels we had just left behind.

I looked around, scanning the area for any signs of danger. There was nothing but the gentle rustling of leaves and the sweet fragrance of the blossoms. It was peaceful, but I couldn't help but feel uneasy. I knew if we kept going, we would be entering the Shadow Lands.

We continued down the path, the soft petals crunching beneath our feet. We came to a small clearing, and my breath hitched at the sight before us.

This was it.

The trees before us began to wither and decay. Their twisted, gnarled branches stretched towards the sky like bony fingers. The once-vibrant pink petals turned black and crumbled beneath our feet. The air grew heavy and thick, and a sense of dread settled over me like a shroud. We had entered the Shadow Lands, and I could feel the darkness closing in around us.

We pressed onward, our weapons at the ready. My heart was pounding in my chest as we stepped further into the dead forest. I knew from what Amara had told me that we couldn't go too much further or we would be stuck inside the barrier.

I tried to call upon my water nymphs, but they still wouldn't surface.

Suddenly, we heard a low growl, and I froze.

We turned to see a massive demon looming over us, its eyes glowing a bright red. This one was slightly different from the ones we'd faced before. Its long, razor-sharp claws glinted in the dim light, and its sharp teeth glimmered with saliva.

My hands shook as I reached for Ben's sword at my side. Xander stepped in front of me, his own sword gleaming in the darkness. The demon let out a deafening screech before charging towards us.

Xander and I stood our ground as the demon bore down on us. Its claws slashed through the air, but we were quick to dodge. Xander's sword whistled through the air as he attacked, but the demon was quick to block every strike.

I watched in horror as Erik was knocked back by the demon's powerful tail, Larina and Victoria rushing to help him up, while Hazel ran to my side.

Taking a deep breath, I closed my eyes and focused on the powers within me. They surged through my veins, giving me the strength I needed to face this demon.

Opening my eyes, I could see the demon charging towards me. I waited until the last possible moment before side stepping out of the way. I swung my arms and called forth a fierce whirlpool, which lifted the demon and slammed it against the ground with a deafening thud.

The demon shrieked, struggling to get back up. Its eyes glowed with fury as it prepared to charge toward me again.

But before it could, a bright light engulfed it. My water nymphs had finally arrived, and they were ready to fight. They moved in perfect harmony as they surrounded the demon, slicing through the demon with their razor-sharp claws. The demon let out an agonizing scream as it was slowly pulled apart by my water nymphs.

A sudden explosion of silver light burst out of me and illuminated the area. It rippled through the air, growing brighter until I could no longer look directly at it. My water nymphs moved forward, bringing with them a wave of pure energy that destroyed the demon in an instant.

I let out a deep breath, feeling the tension leave my body. We did it! *I* did it!

But as the silver light faded away, I felt a deep sense of exhaustion wash over me. My knees buckled, and I collapsed to the ground. Hazel rushed to my side, her hand on my back as she helped me sit up.

"Are you okay?" she asked, concern etched on her face.

I nodded weakly, my breaths coming in short gasps. "I'm fine," I managed to say, though I wasn't sure if I believed it myself.

Xander and the others came over to where we were sitting, their swords still at the ready. "That was incredible," Xander said, a hint of awe in his voice.

I smiled weakly, feeling a sense of pride at what we had just accomplished. But I knew that our journey was far from over. The Shadow Lands were a dangerous place, and we still had a long way to go before we could rescue Amara.

CHAPTER SIXTEEN

Amara

The moonlit garden held a quiet magic as Wesley and I wandered through its winding paths. The scent of blooming flowers filled the air, and the soft rustle of leaves created a soothing melody around us. It was our secret retreat, away from the prying eyes of the palace.

Wesley's laughter, genuine and warm, echoed in the tranquil night. He reached out to pluck a delicate blossom from a nearby bush, presenting it to me with a playful grin.

"For you, milady," he teased, his eyes holding a twinkle that hinted at something more.

I accepted the flower, a smile playing on my lips. "Thank you, kind sir. Your chivalry knows no bounds."

He chuckled, and for a moment, our gazes lingered a fraction longer than usual. It was as if the air between us crackled with unspoken words and shared secrets.

As we strolled through the moonlit garden, Wesley's hand brushed against mine, a subtle touch that spoke volumes. Our fingers intertwined, a silent understanding passing between us. It was a gesture so familiar yet laden with a sweetness that hinted at a deeper connection.

In the quietude of the night, our laughter mingled, creating an invisible thread that bound us together.

Underneath the moon's gentle glow, we found a secluded bench and sat side by side. The air was filled with an unspoken tension, a magnetic pull that drew us closer without the need for words.

As Wesley spoke of mundane things—a tale from the stables, a humorous encounter with the castle staff—the air shimmered with an underlying emotion. It was a dance of unspoken affection, a secret language that only we understood.

The moon cast a soft radiance upon us, and I stole a glance at Wesley. His eyes, the windows to a world he kept hidden, held a warmth that went beyond friendship. In that moment, our connection felt like a carefully guarded secret, a flame flickering in the quiet corners of our hearts.

But just as the moment between us grew more intense, the sound of footsteps approaching shattered our illusion of privacy. We turned to see the Queen herself, her expression stern as she surveyed us with a critical eye.

"Princess Amara, it is late. What are you doing out here?" My mother demanded, her disapproval palpable.

Wesley stood up, his hand slipping out of mine as he gave a respectful bow. "Your Highness, I was just escorting Princess Amara through the gardens."

The Queen's gaze flickered between us, and I felt the heat rise to my cheeks as she scrutinized us. "Princess Amara, I expect you to act with the utmost decorum at all times. Is that clear?"

I lowered my head, feeling the weight of her words bearing down on me. "Yes, Your Highness."

With a final, disapproving glance, my mother turned and walked away, leaving us alone in the moonlit garden once more.

I turned to Wesley, my heart heavy. "I'm sorry," I whispered. "I shouldn't have put you in that position."

Wesley took my hand, his eyes softening. "You have nothing to be sorry for. I'd do anything for you, Amara."

His words stirred something within me—a longing that I couldn't quite name. We sat in silence for a few moments, and I couldn't help but feel a sense of sadness wash over me. I knew that our secret retreats would have to come to an end and that *our connection would have to be buried beneath the weight of royal expectations.*

But for one fleeting moment, I allowed myself to revel in the shared connection, the unspoken love that existed between us. It was a feeling I would carry with me always, even as we were torn apart.

As we stood up and made our way back to the palace, I couldn't help but wonder what the future held for us. Would we ever be able to explore our feelings for each other, or would we be forever confined to the roles society had thrust upon us?

CHAPTER SEVENTEEN

Avery

What little of the sun we could see through the darkness was just beginning to set. Up ahead, I could make out Lieutenant-General McKenna, his sharp burgundy uniform a stark contrast against the dying forest. We suspected that we were at the border. We couldn't tell for sure, but Amara said it wasn't too far into the forest once it started to decay, and we couldn't risk going any further.

McKenna bowed his head to Xander as he stepped forward and readied his sword. "I think it would be best for you all to stay here while my men and I scout out ahead," he said firmly. "We'll rest for the night and then move forward with our plan to enter the Shadow Lands in the morning."

"Just don't go too far," Xander ordered. And with that, McKenna and a few of his soldiers went off in different directions. The remaining soldiers silently went about constructing an evening camp filled with tents and fire pits that illuminated the surrounding darkness.

As the soldiers worked, I sat beside Xander and watched as the sun completely disappeared. The darkness was absolute, and the only sounds were the occasional rustling of leaves. My mind couldn't help but wander to Amara and what she could be going through in the Shadow Lands. I knew we had to rescue her, but the thought of what lay ahead was terrifying.

Xander put his arm around me, pulling me closer. "We'll get her back," he whispered, his voice barely audible over the sounds of the forest. "We'll do whatever it takes."

I nodded, trying to push away the fear and doubt that crept into my mind. We were in this together, and we would not let anything stop us.

As the night wore on, the soldiers settled in for the evening. Some sat by the fire, others rested in their tents, but all were vigilant and ready for whatever the Shadow Lands would throw at them.

I sat with Xander and the others around a fire, trying to distract myself from the looming danger by telling stories and jokes. But no matter how hard I tried, my thoughts always drifted back to Amara.

Just then, a loud rustling caught our attention. We all tensed, reaching for our weapons as we turned towards the noise. But as we peered into the darkness, we saw nothing but the swaying branches of trees.

"It's just the wind," Victoria said, relaxing her grip on her sword.

But I couldn't shake the feeling that something was wrong. I stood up and walked towards the trees, my senses on high alert. The darkness pressed in around me, suffocating and thick.

Suddenly, a sharp pain erupted in my head, and I stumbled backwards. Xander caught me before I fell, his eyes wide with alarm.

"What's wrong?" he asked, his voice shaking.

I clutched at my head, feeling a searing pain pulse through my temples. "I don't know," I gasped. "Something's not right."

Xander helped me back to the fire, where the others were now on high alert. McKenna and his soldiers had returned, their swords at the ready.

"What's going on?" McKenna demanded, surveying the area.

"I don't know," Xander said, his eyes on me. "The Princess is in pain."

I gasped. "It feels like someone's trying to get inside my mind." *Esmeray.* I thought. *Does she already know we're here?*

Xander's grip on my arm tightened. "We need to be on high alert. Something is coming."

Suddenly, a deafening roar filled the air. We all turned towards the sound, our weapons at the ready. Out of the darkness, a massive creature emerged, its eyes glowing with an otherworldly light.

It was a demon, unlike any we had ever seen. Its skin was a sickly grey, and its horns were twisted and gnarled. It towered over us, its massive claws reaching out to grab us.

Without hesitation, Xander charged towards the demon, his sword flashing in the firelight. The demon swiped its claws at him, but Xander dodged out of the way.

I drew on the powers within me, calling forth a blast of water that slammed into the demon's side. The demon roared in pain, but it was far from defeated.

Larina and Victoria joined the fight, slashing at the demon with their swords. The demon retaliated by swinging its massive claws at us, each swipe sending us flying backwards. I hit the ground hard, pain shooting through my body as I struggled to get back up.

McKenna and his soldiers rushed forward, their swords drawn. But the demon seemed to anticipate their moves, sidestepping their attacks with ease.

Hazel ran to my side, offering me a hand. The demon lunged at us, its massive claws aimed straight at our heads.

"No!" Xander shouted as he dove for us, knocking us back to the ground. The demon's claws just missing us. We scrambled to our feet as the demon turned towards Xander. Its eyes locked onto him, and it charged forward with incredible speed. Xander stood his ground, his sword held firmly in his grip.

This demon was too strong; I knew I needed to do something to help. I called upon the power within me again. Trying to summon my water nymphs to help fight against this thing.

But something was wrong. As I focused on my powers, the pain in my head intensified to the point of blinding agony. I could barely stand, let alone control my magic.

The demon was upon Xander, its claws ready to strike. But just as it was about to land the killing blow, a bright light erupted from within the darkness and engulfed the demon. The light was so bright that it took a moment for my eyes to adjust.

When they finally did, I could see a figure standing in the centre of the light. It was a woman with long, dark hair. She wore a long white dress that seemed to glow from within.

"Esmeray," Xander spat, his sword still at the ready.

But the woman didn't seem to pay him any attention. Instead, she turned her gaze towards me, and I felt a chill run down my spine.

"You're the one," she said, her voice ringing with a strange power. "The one who caused all of this."

I shook my head, confusion and fear warring within me. "I don't understand."

Esmeray stepped closer, her eyes fixed on mine. "You have a power within you, Princess," she said. "A power that can change everything. But you are too weak to control it."

I felt a surge of anger rise within me. "I am not weak!" I yelled. "I will not let you take control of me, Esmeray."

The woman laughed, a sound that echoed through the forest. "Oh, my dear princess. You have no choice in the matter. Your fate has already been sealed."

With that, she disappeared into the darkness, leaving us all stunned and confused. The demon was gone too; it vanished as quickly as it had appeared.

Everything was quiet as we all stood there, taking in the reality of the situation. It was evident that we needed to act fast if we wanted any chance of a successful rescue mission and an escape from the Shadow Lands alive. But how could we manage to defeat Esmeray and get to Amara?

Xander stepped forward, his eyes locked on mine. "We need to focus," he said. "Esmeray is powerful, but she's not invincible. We'll find a way to stop her and rescue Amara."

I nodded, drawing on the last of my strength. "I won't let her win," I said, determination filling me. "We'll save Amara, and we'll stop Esmeray. No matter what it takes."

"Amara? Is this not Princess Amara?" McKenna asked, his brows crinkling as his eyes darted between me and Xander.

Xander's jaw clenched as he realized his mistake. We had been so careful up until this point.

I shook my head, biting my lip nervously. We might as well tell them; it would be too difficult to try and hide one of us during our escape. It was time they knew. "Princess Amara is my twin sister. My name is Avery. She is trapped inside the Shadow Lands, and we will do everything in our power to bring her back home safely."

Murmurs broke out around the soldiers, especially the few that had come from Soluna.

McKenna hesitated for a moment before nodding. "Very well. We will do everything in our power to help."

The group rallied around us, ready to face whatever challenges lay ahead. We didn't know what the future held, but we knew one thing for certain—we wouldn't let anyone or anything stand in the way of our mission.

As we set out into the darkness, I felt a new sense of purpose and strength. No matter how dangerous the journey, we would face it with courage. For Amara, for our kingdom, and for ourselves.

The Shadow Lands may have been a place of fear and darkness—one we knew so little about, but we were determined to overcome it. With our swords drawn and our minds focused, we moved forward, ready to face whatever challenges lay ahead. We would not let Esmeray or the Shadow Lands defeat us.

As we walked through the dark forest, we were constantly on high alert, expecting an attack at any moment. We could feel the eyes of unknown beings watching us, but we could never see them. The silence was deafening, broken only by the occasional rustling of leaves or snapping of twigs. It was as if the forest itself was holding its breath, waiting for us to make the wrong move.

Hours passed by, and the closer we got to the heart of the Shadow Lands, the more we could feel the darkness trying to consume us. But we were determined not to let it win. We marched on, our steps slow and steady.

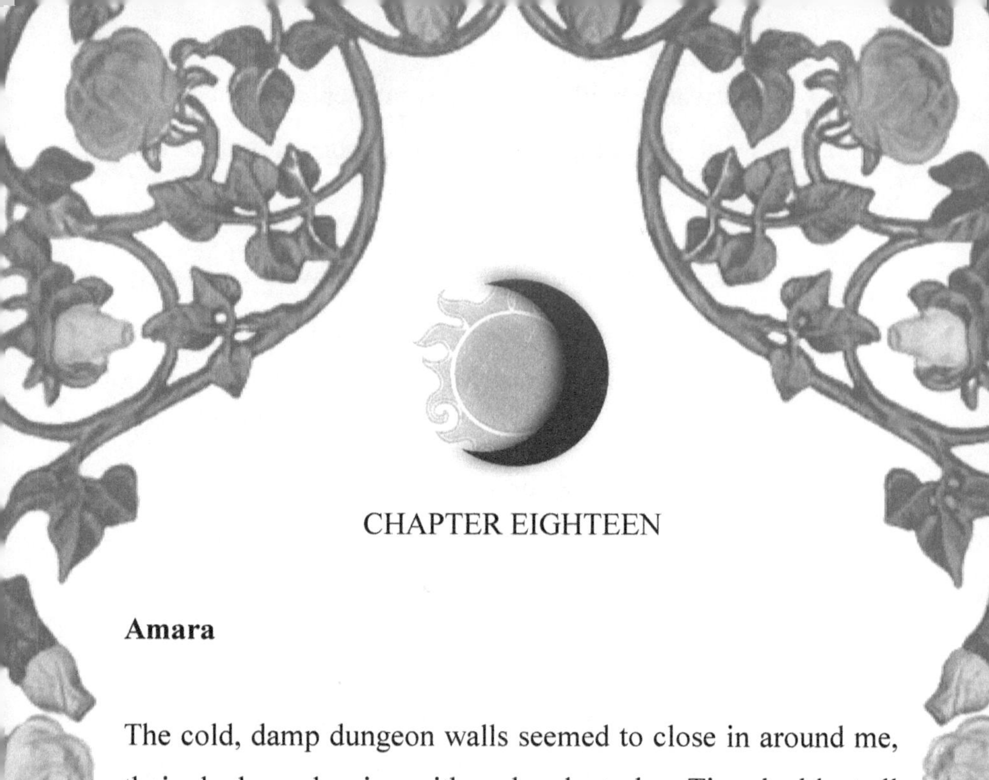

CHAPTER EIGHTEEN

Amara

The cold, damp dungeon walls seemed to close in around me, their shadows dancing with malevolent glee. Time had lost all its meaning. Esmeray had moved me, and the chains that bound me to the frigid stone floor clinked with each strained movement. It seemed my captor revelled in tormenting me, a sadistic puppeteer orchestrating the dance of my despair.

Wesley stood guard over me as if he were a puppet on Esmeray's strings. His eyes, once warm with the glow of friendship, now held a distant emptiness that sent shivers down my spine. I could sense the conflict within him—the struggle between the memories of our bond and the dark influence that gripped his soul.

I knew that he was not entirely lost, that there was still a chance for him to break free from Esmeray's control. But how could I reach him? How could I convince him to fight against this?

The sound of footsteps echoed through the dungeon, pulling me from my thoughts. I looked up to see Esmeray approaching, her familiar green eyes fixed on me. She wore a smile that made my skin crawl, like a predator stalking its prey.

"Hello, Princess," she said, her voice silky and smooth. "How are you enjoying your stay in my humble abode?"

I spat at her as she came closer, but the spit only landed on the ground in front of me. The chains that bound me made it impossible to move any closer to her.

Esmeray laughed, her eyes flashing with amusement. "Feisty, aren't we? I like that. It makes the game so much more fun."

"What game?" I demanded, my voice shaking with anger and fear.

Esmeray circled around me, her fingers trailing along the chains that held me in place. "The game of power, Princess. I have plans for Soluna—plans that involve you and your sister. And I have no intention of letting anyone or anything stand in my way."

My heart sank at her words. What could we do against someone with such immense power? But I refused to give up hope. "You won't win," I said, struggling against the chains. "Soluna will stand strong against you, and we will defeat you."

Esmeray chuckled, her eyes gleaming with malice. "Oh, my dear princess. You have so much to learn about the world and the power dynamics at play. But don't worry. You'll learn soon enough."

With that, she turned on her heel and left the dungeon, leaving me alone with Wesley.

I stared at him, willing him to look at me and see the truth in my eyes. But he remained stoic, his gaze fixed on the ground. I couldn't give up on him. I had to try.

"Wesley," I said, my voice barely above a whisper. "Please, you have to fight against her. You know me. You know who I am. You know what's right."

He didn't say anything, but I saw a flicker of emotion in his eyes. Hope blossomed within me.

"You can do this," I said, my voice stronger now. "I believe in you. We can defeat her together."

For a moment, it seemed like he might speak, like the person I knew was still there. But then his eyes grew distant again, and he turned away from me.

I felt tears prickle at the corners of my eyes, but I refused to let them fall. I couldn't give up on him. I wouldn't.

Closing my eyes, I drew on the last of my strength. I needed to find a way to break free from these chains and show Wesley that there was still hope. As I focused, a glimmer of light appeared in front of me, growing brighter by the second until it formed into a small ball of fire.

I gasped, surprised by the sudden appearance of the flame. It flickered and danced in the air, seeming to beckon me forward.

Without hesitation, I leaned toward it, letting the heat wash over me. It was comforting and familiar. And then it vanished, and the cell turned pitch black.

For a moment, I panicked, wondering if Esmeray had found some way to extinguish the flame, but then I heard a soft whisper in my ear. *"Keep going, Amara. You're closer than you think."* Calypso's familiar voice sang.

Opening my eyes, I searched for her. But there was no one there, at least not that I could see. The darkness was complete, except for the small pinprick of light that had appeared once more.

I focused on the flame, willing it to grow larger to illuminate the room around me. And to my surprise, it worked. The ball of fire grew into a roaring inferno, casting a warm light across the dungeon. And there, standing before me, was Wesley.

His eyes were wide, and his mouth was agape. I could see the struggle within him—the fight between the darkness and the light. But I knew that I had to act quickly before Esmeray returned.

"Wesley, please," I said, my voice shaking with emotion. "You have to fight against her. You have to remember who you are."

He seemed to hesitate for a moment, his eyes flickering between me and the flames. "I remember who you are, just fine. You're the woman I loved who left me here to rot."

"That's not how it happened!" I cried.

Wesley's expression remained cold and unforgiving. "Isn't it? You left me, Amara. You left me to die in this hellhole while you went off to live your life as a princess. You chose your kingdom over me, like you always did."

"I had no choice," I pleaded. "I had to leave to protect Soluna, to protect *you*."

Wesley scoffed, shaking his head. "Protect me? You *abandoned* me. And now you expect me to help you? To fight against the woman who saved me from this place?"

"She didn't save you, Wesley," I said, my voice steady. "She's using you, manipulating you, controlling you. Can't you see that? You're not yourself. You're not the man I know."

Wesley's expression softened slightly, but I could see the battle still raging within him. "I don't know what to believe anymore."

"Believe in us," I said, reaching out to him. "Believe in our friendship, in the love I had and still have for you."

Wesley hesitated for a moment longer before taking a step closer to me. His eyes searched mine, looking for any hint of deceit or manipulation. But all he saw was the truth—the raw emotion that I had been holding back.

"I want to believe you, Amara," he said, his voice barely above a whisper. "But I don't know if I can."

"You can," I said firmly, taking his hand in mine. "We can do this together. We can fight against Esmeray and win. But you have to choose to come back to us."

Wesley looked down at our hands, then back up at me. "I don't know if I'm strong enough."

"You are," I said, squeezing his hand. "You're stronger than you know."

My entire being ached for him as I moved my free hand up to caress his cheek, willing him to feel all my longing and desperation for him to return. Every fibre of my being pleaded for him to come back to me, to the person he used to be before. I pressed my forehead against his, willing it to touch his soul and bring him back.

The golden hues of the setting sun painted the sky as I sat on the roof of the stables, a place that held the memories of countless stolen moments with Wesley. It had become our sanctuary, a place where laughter and shared glances could exist beyond the constraints of our societal roles.

Wesley and I had always been inseparable, our connection transcending the boundaries set by our disparate worlds. As the princess, I was expected to uphold the dignity and expectations that came with my title. Wesley, on the other hand, was a stable boy—his days filled with the rigours of training to join the royal guard.

Yet, as we sat on the quiet rooftop of the stables, none of those distinctions mattered. We were simply Amara and Wesley, two souls entwined in a friendship that felt like something more.

As I gazed out at the breathtaking beauty of the sunset, I felt a rush of emotions wash over me. The vibrant colours mirrored the conflicting emotions swirling within me. I watched as Wesley skillfully tended to the horses below, his every movement a testament to the dedication he poured into his training.

I climbed down, desperate to be closer to him and to talk to him. Though I'd never let him know.

Wesley turned, a smile playing on his lips as he wiped sweat from his brow.

"Princess," he greeted, a respectful nod accompanying his words.

I rolled my eyes, a playful smirk gracing my face. "Wes, how many times have I told you to drop the formalities when it's just the two of us?"

He chuckled, the sound resonating within me. "Old habits die hard, Your Highness."

Our gazes locked, and for a moment, time seemed to stand still. In that suspended instant, the weight of our respective stations felt like distant echoes. It was just Amara and Wesley.

He finished up his work, and we made our way to the gardens. We walked side by side, the garden becoming a witness to the unspoken words that hung in the air. I watched the play of emotions on Wesley's face—fleeting glances that lingered a moment too long, the subtle touch when he helped me over a small stone bridge.

As we reached a secluded alcove, the sun dipped below the horizon, casting long shadows that danced along the stone walls. Wesley leaned against the moss-covered bricks, his gaze meeting mine in a silent exchange that held the weight of our unspoken truths.

"You'll make a magnificent queen one day," he said, his voice carrying a hint of both admiration and resignation.

I sighed, the weight of my responsibilities pressing down on me. "I never asked for this. I never wanted to be queen. I just want to be Amara."

Wesley's eyes softened, a silent understanding passing between us. "And I just want to be Wesley—the one who walks beside you, not behind you."

As the evening deepened, we lingered in the garden, caught in a dance of shared moments and unspoken dreams. The moon ascended to take its place in the night sky, casting a soft glow upon the garden—a silent testament to the secrets we kept and the yearning that pulsed within the quiet corners of our hearts.

"Walk beside me, Wesley," I breathed.

And then, without warning, Wesley leaned forward, closing the small space between us, and pressed his lips to mine. It was a desperate, passionate kiss, filled with all the love and longing that had been building between us for so long. For a moment, we were lost in the heat of the moment, the desire consuming us both. But then Wesley pulled away, his eyes searching mine.

"I'm sorry," he said, his voice thick with emotion.

Footsteps echoed through the dungeon once more, followed by a slow clap. I turned to find Esmeray watching us in the doorway. An evil grin spread widely across her face.

"Well, isn't this just lovely?" Esmeray mocked, her eyes glinting with amusement. "The princess and her former lover reunited in the most romantic of settings. How touching."

I pulled away from Wesley, my heart racing with fear. I knew that Esmeray had seen everything, and I didn't know what she would do next.

Esmeray stepped closer, her eyes locked on Wesley. "I have to admit, I'm surprised. I thought you were loyal to me, Wesley. But it seems that the princess still holds some sway over you."

Wesley's expression hardened. "I'm not a pawn in your game, Esmeray. I have my own mind, my own will."

Esmeray chuckled, shaking her head. "That's where you're wrong, my dear. You belong to me. I own your mind, your will, your very soul. And I will not tolerate any disobedience."

I watched in horror as Esmeray lifted a hand, a dark energy crackling around her fingers. "But don't worry, Wesley. I won't kill you just yet. You still have some use to me."

Esmeray turned towards me; her lips curled into a cruel smile. "As for you, my dear princess, I think it's time we had a little chat."

I braced myself for whatever was to come next, knowing that Esmeray's wrath would be swift and brutal. But as she stepped towards me, a sudden burst of energy surged through my body, tingling in my fingertips and coursing through my veins.

Looking down, I was amazed to see the flames dancing around my hands, burning hot and bright. I could feel their power, their strength, and I knew that I had to use it. Without hesitation, I lifted my hands towards Esmeray, summoning all the fire within me.

The flames shot towards her, engulfing her in a fierce inferno. But to my surprise, she didn't scream or cry out in pain. She laughed.

"You think fire can hurt me, little princess?" Esmeray taunted from within the flames. "I am a creature of darkness, born of the shadows. Fire cannot harm me."

The flames began to die down, leaving Esmeray unscathed. She stepped out of them, turning her attention towards me once more. "But you do have potential, my dear. Such power within you. I could use that."

I backed away from her, fear gripping my heart. But Esmeray was relentless, her eyes glowing with a dark energy. "Join me, Amara. Together, we can rule Soluna. Together, we can destroy anyone who stands in our way."

I shook my head, refusing to give in to her temptations. "I will never join you, Esmeray. I will always fight against you."

Esmeray's expression turned cold and angry. "Then you leave me no choice. I will destroy you once and for all."

With a wave of her hand, Esmeray summoned a wave of dark energy that slammed into me, knocking me to the ground. I struggled to get up, but the energy held me down, crushing me with its weight.

Esmeray stepped closer, a wicked grin on her face. "You see, Amara, you're no match for me. You may have some power, but I am far stronger. And soon, you will understand that."

Gritting my teeth, I pushed against the energy with all my might. I could feel the fire within me, burning hot and bright. It was then that I realized what I had to do.

I summoned all the fire within me, using it to break free from the energy's hold. The flames consumed the energy, burning it away until nothing was left.

Esmeray's eyes widened in surprise, but she quickly regained her composure. "Impressive, princess. But it won't save you."

My eyes flicked over her shoulder. She had Wesley pinned to one of the stone walls of my cell with her shadow magic. Next to him sat the only candle in my room. I had to do something fast. Fire couldn't destroy her, but if I used my telekinesis, I could at least slow her down.

Summoning every ounce of power I had, I sent the heavy iron candle holder hurtling through the air towards Esmeray; it collided with a loud clang against the back of her head. She tottered forward, releasing Wesley from her grip as she crumpled to the ground.

I scrambled to my feet, running towards Wesley as he stumbled towards me. We helped each other up, looking down at Esmeray as she lay motionless on the ground.

For a moment, everything was quiet. But then a sudden surge of energy rippled through the dungeon. The walls began to shake, dust falling from the ceiling.

"We have to get out of here," I said, my voice filled with urgency.

We turned back to Esmeray just as her body disappeared into a cloud of smoke. I knew this was far from over. It would take a lot more than a candleholder to defeat her. She would come back stronger and harder to defeat us. But for now, we had to get out of the dungeon and figure out our next move.

The dungeon trembled around us, echoing the intensity of the confrontation that had just taken place. Wesley's gaze remained fixed on the dissipating smoke where Esmeray had vanished, his eyes clouded with torment. As the dust settled, the reality of the situation crashed down on him.

"I hurt you," he whispered, his voice choked with remorse. "I hurt you so much."

The weight of his realization hung heavily in the air. I reached for his trembling hands, trying to ground him in the present. "Wesley, it wasn't you. It was her. She manipulated you, twisted your mind. None of that was your fault."

He looked at me with anguish etched across his face. "I remember it all, Amara. Every moment I tormented you, every cruel word I said. I can't... I can't live with what I've done."

Tears welled up in his eyes, mirroring the pain that echoed within my own heart. I pulled him into a desperate embrace, as if I could shield him from the torment that threatened to consume him.

"We have to leave, Wesley," I urged, my voice firm. "We can't stay here. Esmeray will come back, and the dungeon might collapse on us. We need to find a way out."

He nodded, a numbness settling over him as he allowed me to guide him toward the exit. The tunnels were narrow, the walls closing in around us as if to suffocate the air itself. My mind raced, searching for a way to escape the encroaching danger.

As we stumbled through the winding passages, the ominous creaking of stone echoed through the labyrinthine corridors. I cast a wary glance back, realizing the dungeon was on the verge of collapse. The urgency propelled us forward, our steps quickening with each passing moment.

Esmeray's taunting voice resonated in the distance. "You can't escape, Amara. I'm always one step ahead."

The threat hung in the air, but we pressed on, fueled by the desperate need for freedom. The twists and turns of the tunnels blurred into a disorienting maze, our senses heightened by the impending danger.

The complete darkness that had previously engulfed us suddenly gave way to a small, faint flicker of light. Our weary eyes followed its source, and we were met with the sight of a heavy wooden door blocking our way. We stood for a moment, too exhausted to move, until the shock of realization hit us: the only way out of this place was through it.

A terrifying sight greeted us as we burst through the door. The prisoners huddled together; their faces paled with terror as we stumbled into the room. They were crammed in cages of iron bars, with barely enough space for them to stand. We could see the desperation on their faces as they held onto each other for comfort.

One of the prisoners called out to us, his voice trembling with fear. "Please, help us," he begged, his hands reaching out through the bars of his cage.

"We have to help them," I said, turning to Wesley.

He nodded, understanding the gravity of the situation. He searched around the room for something to break the locks.

The heat of my flames built up inside me once more, but I knew that this time it wasn't enough. We needed more than just fire to break these cages.

As Wesley searched, I turned my attention towards the cages themselves. I could see that they were made of metal, locked tight with heavy padlocks. But there was something strange about them—something I couldn't quite put my finger on.

And then it hit me. These cages weren't just made of metal. They were made of shadow.

I reached out towards the nearest cage, my fingers brushing against the bars. At first, I felt nothing. But then a sudden surge of energy rippled through me, and I could feel the shadow magic coursing through the metal bars.

With a deep breath, I summoned all the power within me, using it to break the shadows that bound the cages together. The metal bars fell apart, clanging to the ground as the cages opened wide.

The prisoners scrambled to their feet while Wesley grabbed bags and weapons that had been thrown to the opposite side of the room. He handed each of us some sort of sword or axe and handed me one of the few satchels he had found.

The others followed us as we ran towards the exit. The walls continued to shake, dust and debris falling from the ceiling. But we didn't stop, pushing ourselves to the limit as we raced towards the light at the end of the tunnel.

As we burst out into the fresh air, the sound of alarms blared behind us. Esmeray's soldiers and demons were hot on our heels, but we didn't stop running. We had to get as far away as possible to find a safe place to regroup and plan our next move.

Wesley led us through the twisting streets of a crumbling village, his familiarity with the area allowing us to dodge the guards and slip through alleys without being seen. We stopped briefly to catch our breath, looking around us for any sign of danger. The prisoners huddled close to us, their eyes wide with fear and gratitude.

"Thank you," one of them said. His voice cracked with emotion as he looked me in the eyes. "Thank you for saving us." I thought about what he was asking and knew that we couldn't just leave them here; we had to help them. They had nowhere to go, no one to turn to.

Then I remembered something. Esmeray was after Celestials. They may have special gifts that could help us.

Turning back toward the group, I asked, "Do any of you have any special powers or abilities?"

At first, they looked at me with confusion etched on their faces, but then one of them spoke up.

"Most of us are Celestials. However, Esmeray has stolen our gifts from the gods," she said softly, her voice barely above a whisper.

My heart sank at the thought of Esmeray possessing such power. But then an idea struck me.

"What if we could get your gifts back?" I asked, turning to face the group.

Their eyes widened in surprise at the suggestion, but then hope flickered in their gazes.

"Do any of you know where Esmeray is keeping the gifts?" I asked, my voice low and urgent.

The prisoners looked at each other, whispering amongst themselves. Finally, one of them stepped forward, her eyes filled with determination.

"I overheard one of the guards talking about a room in her shadow palace where Esmeray keeps all the stolen gifts. It's heavily guarded, but if we could get in there, we might be able to take them back."

I nodded, a plan forming in my mind. We had to get into that room, no matter what it took. With the gifts in our possession, we might finally have a chance at defeating Esmeray once and for all.

"Okay, here's what we're going to do," I began, my voice firm and steady. "We're going to gather as much information as we can about Esmeray and her palace. We'll scout the area and find the best way to break in."

The prisoners looked at me with determination in their eyes, ready to fight for their freedom and their gifts. Wesley nodded his approval, his eyes gleaming with excitement at the thought of taking down Esmeray once and for all.

Together, we set our sights on the shadow palace, determined to take back what was rightfully ours.

As we made our way towards the palace, a sense of unease settled over me. Esmeray was powerful, and we were going up against her in her own stronghold. But we had no other choice. We had to stop her, no matter the cost.

We had to be careful not to attract too much attention. Wesley led us through the twisting streets, staying close to the shadows and avoiding any well-lit areas, which was easy considering where we were. We moved as one, like a group of shadows ourselves, our determination the only light that guided us.

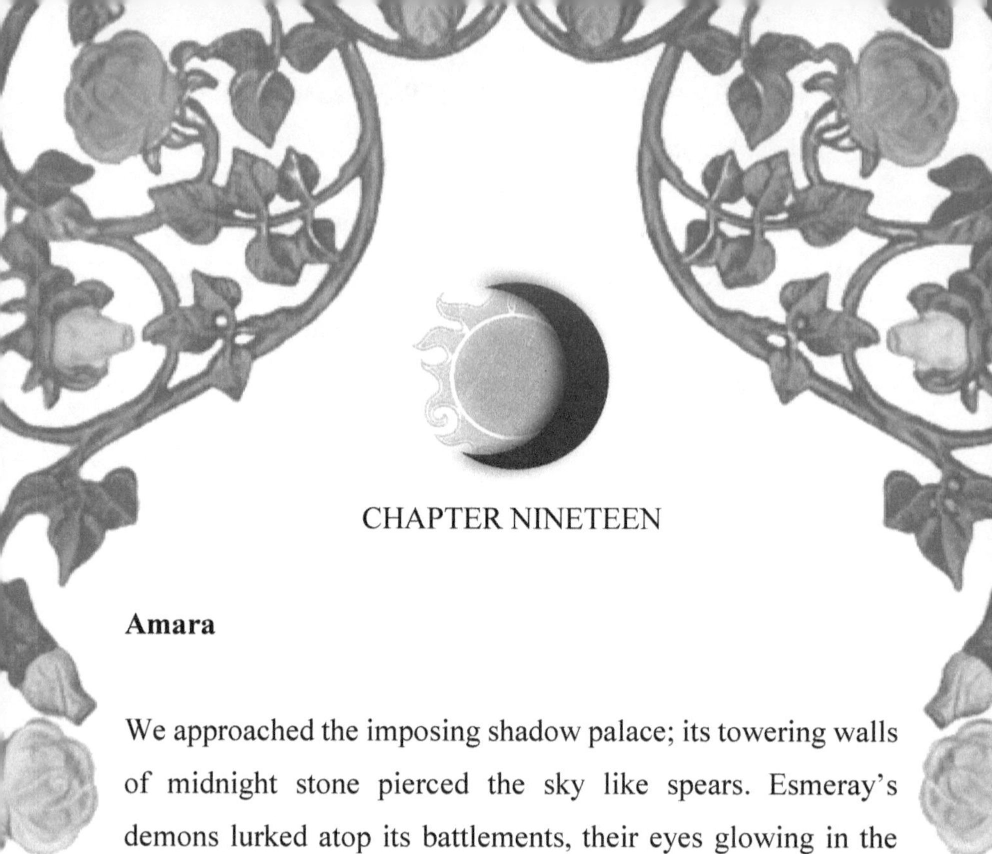

CHAPTER NINETEEN

Amara

We approached the imposing shadow palace; its towering walls of midnight stone pierced the sky like spears. Esmeray's demons lurked atop its battlements, their eyes glowing in the eerie half-light.

A shiver ran down my spine as we crept closer, the weight of all the lives we were fighting for heavy on my shoulders. This was it—the final showdown. I could feel the magic coursing through my veins—a hum of power that echoed the beat of my heart.

Wesley led us to a hidden entrance—a small door tucked away in the shadows, barely visible unless you knew where to look. He whispered a spell, and the door creaked open, revealing a dark, narrow passage.

"That's our way in," he said, his voice barely above a whisper.

The prisoners looked at each other nervously, but I could see the determination in their eyes. They were ready to fight for their freedom and their gifts.

Wesley moved to enter the passageway, but I stopped him, my hand on his shoulder. "Wait."

"What is it?" he asked, his brows knitted together.

"Should we really all go in there? What if it's a trap? I think an even smaller group of us should go in while the rest wait here."

Wesley considered my words before nodding in agreement. "You're right. It's too dangerous to bring everyone in. We'll need a small, stealthy team to sneak in and retrieve the gifts."

I turned to the group of prisoners, looking for volunteers. Several hands went up, eager to help in any way they could. I selected three Celestials, the ones who seemed the most capable and willing to do whatever it took to get their gifts back.

"Okay," I said, my voice low and urgent. "You three are coming with me. The rest of you stay here and keep watch with Wesley. If anything happens, make a run for it."

The prisoners nodded, their eyes filled with fear and determination. It was a risky move, but we had no other choice.

We needed those gifts if we were going to defeat Esmeray and free all the prisoners from her hold.

"What? You don't want me to come with you?" Wesley asked, a hurt expression crossing his face.

I shook my head. "No, Wes. You're in charge of keeping the others safe and making sure we have a way out if things go wrong. We need you out here."

He nodded, understanding the importance of his role. "Just…be safe."

I locked eyes with Wesley, my heart racing as I felt the warmth of his hand on my wrist. His gaze was intense, searching for something, and I held it until I finally gave him a slight nod. As I began to turn away, his grip tightened, stopping me in my tracks. His eyes were still fixed on mine, and I wasn't sure what he wanted from me.

Wesley stepped closer, his light brown eyes twinkling. My breath caught in my throat as he raised his hands to cup my face and leaned down to capture my lips with his. My body quivered against his strong arms, which had wound around me.

I melted into his kiss, the heat of him radiating through my body. The world around us disappeared as we lost ourselves in the moment, his hands roaming over my curves.

But then a cough from one of the prisoners broke the spell, and we pulled apart, our breathing ragged. Wesley looked into my eyes, his expression soft and tender.

"Why do I feel like every time we say goodbye, it could be our last?" he whispered.

"It won't be," I promised.

"I love you," he breathed, his voice raw with emotion.

"I love you too," I replied, my heart racing.

We pulled away from each other, both of us breathing heavily. Wesley gave me a smile before turning to the others, his expression serious once again.

"Alright, let's do this," he said, his voice steady and firm.

I watched him go. I couldn't let my feelings for him distract me from the task at hand.

We slipped inside, the darkness enveloping us like a cloak. The only light came from the pale, eerie glow of the crystals that lined the walls, casting jagged shadows across the rough-hewn stone. We moved quietly, our footsteps barely making a sound on the stone floor.

"What are your names?" I asked softly, figuring it would be useful to have something to call each of them.

The Celestials looked at each other nervously before the one on my left spoke up. "I am Lyra," she said, her voice barely above a whisper.

The one in the middle cleared her throat before speaking. "I'm Twila," she said, her voice stronger than Lyra's.

"And I'm Bastian," the one on my right said, his voice deep and steady.

I nodded, committing their names to memory. "Alright, Lyra, Twila, and Bastian. Let's find that room and get those gifts back."

We moved through the palace, avoiding any guards and demons we came across. The corridors were twisting and dark, making it difficult to navigate, but we pressed on.

Finally, we came to a heavily guarded door, runes etched into its surface pulsing with dark energy. I could feel the power radiating off it and knew that this was the room. This was where Esmeray kept all the stolen gifts.

We flattened ourselves against the cold stone wall and peered around the corner; they hadn't spotted us.

"Any chance any of you know any spells or anything that could remove whatever those runes are?" I asked hopefully.

Twila peeked out from behind her shoulder-length brown hair and spoke. "No, but even if we did, we don't have our magic to do it." She paused for a moment, placing a reassuring hand on my shoulder. "Just focus all your energy on dissolving the runes."

Taking a deep breath, I felt the magic that coursed through my veins like a living thing. Focusing all my energy on the runes, I closed my eyes. Calypso's voice called to me.

Clearing my mind, I focused on the light and power inside me. The air crackled with energy as the runes began to glow brighter, but then, with a sudden burst of light, they vanished. The only issue was that the guards and demons noticed.

They rushed towards us, snarling and brandishing their weapons. Lyra was the first to act, drawing her sword and charging towards the approaching horde. Twila and Bastian followed closely behind.

Summoning what was left of my magic, I raised my arm, and a glowing light burst from me, penetrating each demon one by one until their screams of terror filled the air. My power tore them apart from within—an unstoppable force that only I could control.

The others took care of the two guards that had been stationed there. With the guards and demons defeated, we stepped into the room, and I gasped at what I saw.

I had seen this room before, in my dreams. I'd seen Esmeray, cloaked as the Shadow Lord. And now, as I stood in it, the reality of it all overwhelmed me. The room was small, and the stone walls were carved with even more intricate runes and symbols that pulsed around us. In the centre of the room was a pedestal with an old grimoire I remembered seeing in one of those dreams.

As I approached the pedestal, the grimoire seemed to hum with an ancient power. I reached out to touch it, and a jolt ran through my body. The grimoire glowed brighter, and I felt a surge of energy coursing through me.

"Be careful," Twila warned. "That book could be cursed."

I nodded, knowing that she was right. I studied the grimoire, trying to decipher its contents. It was filled with dark magic and ancient spells, some of which I recognized from Liliana's books.

"We need to get out of here," Bastian said, his voice low and urgent. "Esmeray could be back at any moment."

I nodded, knowing he was right. I turned to find shelves lined with trinkets, jewellery, books, weapons, and more. All of them glowed with a faint, eerie light, and I knew that they had all been imbued with dark magic.

"Over here," Lyra called.

She stood before a large, ornate chest. This must have been where she kept the stolen gifts.

Approaching the chest cautiously, I placed my hands on it, my magic probing its surface. With a sudden burst of energy, the chest opened.

My heart stopped as I saw the gifts of my fellow prisoners, each one glowing with its own unique magic. They were like little orbs of light.

Bastian strode over to where I stood. He squatted down and ran an assessing eye over it before directing his gaze up at me and asking, "How heavy is this thing?"

I shrugged. "Give it a try."

Bastian grunted as he lifted the chest, his muscles bulging with effort. "It's heavy, but I can manage."

"Good," I replied, my eyes scanning the room once more. "Let's get out of here before Esmeray shows up."

As the others slipped out, my eyes caught the grimoire once more. I ran over, grabbed it, and stuffed it into my satchel.

We retraced our steps. And as we made our way back through the winding corridors, I breathed out a sigh of relief. We had succeeded in our mission to retrieve the stolen gifts, and now we could return them to their rightful owners.

Esmeray could be anywhere, and we were still deep within her territory. But I kept my fear at bay, knowing that we had to keep moving forward. Once the Celestials had their powers back, we would be one step closer to defeating her for good.

We emerged from the palace, the night air cool against our skin. The stars twinkled overhead, a reminder of the world beyond the darkness of the Shadow Lands.

"Wesley and the others should be around here somewhere," I muttered.

"Unless something happened to them," Twila said.

"Not helpful." I shot her a glare, and she shrugged a single shoulder.

We walked around the perimeter of the palace, keeping an eye out for any sign of them. Just as I was starting to worry that they had been captured, a voice called out from the shadows.

"Over here!"

We turned to see Wesley and the rest of our group emerge from the darkness. They looked battered and bruised, but alive.

"Thank the gods, you're okay," I said, relief flooding through me.

"What happened?" Bastian asked, his eyes scanning each of them for injuries.

"We were ambushed," Wesley said, his jaw set in a grim line. "Esmeray and her minions caught us off guard. But we managed to fight them off and escape."

I nodded, feeling a sense of pride in my team. We were survivors, and we were fighters. We would do whatever it took to win this war.

"Let's get out of here," I said, motioning for the others to follow me. "We have what we came for, and it's time to return these gifts."

As we made our way further away from Esmeray's shadow palace in search of a safe place to hide out, I couldn't help but think about the grimoire I had taken. It was filled with dark magic, but it was also filled with ancient knowledge. Knowledge that could help us defeat Esmeray once and for all.

I knew that I needed to study it carefully to unlock its secrets and use it to our advantage. But I also knew that the power it held could be dangerous and that I needed to be careful with how I used it.

We walked for hours, our pace slow and cautious. But as we did, I couldn't help but feel a sense of unease settle over me. The power that had surged through me in the shadow palace was still humming beneath my skin, and I knew that there was a darkness within me that I had never fully explored.

"Are you okay?" Wesley asked, his hand coming to rest on my shoulder.

I nodded but couldn't bring myself to speak. I felt as though I was on the edge of a precipice, ready to fall into the unknown.

We stumbled upon a clearing in the dark woods and set up camp. Bastian and Lyra quickly got to work, searching the forest floor for anything dry enough to burn. They scoured every inch of the area, but it seemed like all they found were leaves and twigs that had long since gone rotten. But they managed to gather enough wood to get us through the night. I lit up the small pile of sticks with my fire magic, and we all settled in for the night, tired and weary from the day's events.

I sat apart from the others, pulling the grimoire from my bag and opening it to the first page. The text was written in an ancient language, but somehow, I understood it as if it had been written in my own tongue.

The spells and incantations were dark, but I knew that they could be used for good if wielded properly.

As I read on, I stumbled upon a section that made my blood run cold. It was a spell for summoning a powerful demon, one that could grant immense power to the caster but at a great cost. I closed the grimoire, feeling a cold sweat break out on my forehead. I knew that I couldn't risk using such a spell, no matter how desperate our situation might become.

Looking around at the others, huddled around the fire, I felt as though the weight of the world was on my shoulders. We were in the middle of a war, fighting against a powerful enemy who had already defeated us once before. And if we were going to stand a chance of winning, we needed every advantage we could get.

CHAPTER TWENTY

Avery

Things didn't exactly go according to plan. We had already entered the barrier of the Shadow Lands. We had no idea where Amara or any other prisoners were being kept. We didn't know how we would leave the barrier. The only thing we did know, was that we had to find them and defeat Esmeray. And hopefully, once we did, the barrier would fall.

We spent the next few days wandering through the Shadow Lands, searching for any signs of life or magic. Every step we took was cautious, as we never knew what kind of darkness lurked around us.

I was still unable to summon my water nymphs, but I tried to use my telepathy to search for anyone around us. It also didn't go well; the only people I could pick up were the large group with us. I was grateful to have so many soldiers with us, from both Soluna and Coldoria, but it made this gift more difficult to use and control.

I constantly had to fight against my power, reaching out and overhearing the thoughts of everyone. My head throbbed from so many unwanted thoughts swirling inside my head. I rubbed at my temples, urging the pain and thoughts to go away.

"What's on your mind?" Xander's deep voice asked as he crept up beside me.

Glancing around to make sure no one else was close enough to hear me, I mumbled, "Everyone else's thoughts."

"I'm sorry, maybe you need a distraction," he suggested.

"No, I need to focus on finding Amara."

Xander nodded, his eyes scanning our surroundings. "We'll find her," he said with confidence. "We have to."

I gave him a small smile, grateful for his reassurance. As we continued on, I couldn't help but feel a sense of dread settle in the pit of my stomach. What if we couldn't find Amara? What if we were too late? The thought of her being trapped in this dark and dangerous place was almost too much to bear.

As we trudged through the dark forest, I suddenly heard a faint whisper in the breeze. At first, I thought it was someone within our group's thoughts again, but then I heard it again. I turned to Xander, my eyes wide with excitement.

"Do you hear that?" I asked, pointing in the direction of the sound.

He listened for a moment, then shook his head.

"It… It sounds like Calypso's voice," I said, and without another word, I sprinted in that direction.

"Avery, wait!" Xander shouted as he ran after me.

We pushed through the dense underbrush, the whispers growing louder and more distinct. *"Avery."* Her voice called to me, urging me forward. And then I saw her.

But it wasn't Calypso.

Amara stood with a small group of people, swords raised, ready to take on whatever threat they thought was coming.

She had managed to escape from wherever she had been held captive and was now standing in front of us. Tears of relief sprang to my eyes as I rushed towards her and embraced her tightly.

Xander stood back while we embraced, giving us a moment of privacy. Once we separated, Amara looked exhausted but relieved that we had found her. "You came for me," she murmured.

"You already escaped," I pointed out the obvious.

"I did, but I have no idea how to get out of here," she explained, her voice barely above a whisper.

"We'll find a way out," Xander said, stepping forward. "We'll get you all out of here."

Amara nodded, a small smile on her face. "I knew you would come for me," she said, turning back to me.

We quickly filled Amara in on our plan to defeat Esmeray and bring down the barrier. She listened closely, her eyes flickering with hope.

"I think we need to work together to defeat her, and then hopefully, once she is gone, the barrier will be too."

She nodded. "That makes sense; I'll help however I can."

Suddenly, a bright light flashed around us, blinding us momentarily. When I opened my eyes, everyone else was gone. Amara and I stood alone in the dream-like world from before. A silver glow shimmered before us; my face crinkled as I wondered what the heck was happening.

Calypso materialized before us.

"You brought me to her, didn't you?" I breathed, and Calypso nodded.

"Thank you," Amara said.

Calypso smiled warmly at us both. "I'm just glad you're safe. But there's something else you need to know."

"What can we do?" I asked, the desperation in my tone clear.

"There is a spell that can weaken Esmeray. It's dangerous, but it's our only hope. I've been waiting for someone who has the power to wield it."

"What do we have to do?" Amara asked, stepping forward.

Calypso took a deep breath. "The spell requires a sacrifice. A life must be given in order to weaken Esmeray enough for us to defeat her."

My heart sank. "A sacrifice? I'm not sacrificing someone."

Calypso's gaze flickered between us. "It can't be anyone from the mortal world. It has to be someone from the spirit world, someone who is willing. I want you to use me. My life was lost long ago; this needs to be done. Esmeray is my shadow-self. She is a part of me; if you sacrifice me, you will set me free and weaken Esmeray in the process."

Amara and I exchanged glances, both unsure of what to do. The idea of sacrificing someone, even if it wasn't from the mortal world, was still unsettling. But if it was the only way to defeat Esmeray and bring down the barrier, we had to consider it.

"Calypso, are you sure about this?" I asked, my voice barely above a whisper.

Calypso nodded solemnly. "I've been waiting for this moment for centuries. It's the only way to set things right and restore balance to the world. Think of it as setting me free; I'll be reunited with my sister."

Amara stepped forward, her eyes determined. "We'll do it. But we have to make sure it works. We can't lose you for nothing."

Calypso smiled, her eyes shining with gratitude. "Thank you. I trust you both to carry out the spell."

We spent the next few days preparing for the spell. We didn't need to gather any ingredients or anything like that, luckily. We just needed enough people to surround us in a circle while we cast the spell. Calypso taught us the words for the spell; it was in some ancient language I couldn't understand, but we finally felt as ready as we could.

I was pleasantly surprised that not a single person had questioned Amara. She clearly had more experience with commanding others, and the respect they had for her showed.

With a heavy heart, we prepared for the spell. The group of soldiers from Soluna and Coldoria had joined us as they circled around us. Amara and I held hands while Calypso stood between us, her eyes closed and a serene expression on her face.

Amara and I began chanting the ancient words, our voices low and steady. As we continued, the air around us began to hum with energy. A surge of power rushed through me, and I knew that it was working.

The hairs on my arms stood on end as the spell began to take hold. Calypso's body began to glow with a silver light, her hair whipping around her face as the spell consumed her. A sense of sadness overcame me as I realized that we were about to lose someone who had helped us so much in our journey.

As the spell reached its climax, Calypso's body began to disintegrate into a silver mist. The mist enveloped us, and I felt the power of the magic surge through me and Amara. We chanted louder, pouring all of our energy into the spell.

Finally, with a loud burst of power, the mist dissipated into nothingness. We collapsed to the ground, exhausted but relieved. We had done it.

As we caught our breath and tried to process what had just happened, we looked around and saw that the barrier had finally fallen. The sky was blue, and the sun shone brightly above us.

Everyone around us cheered, but as I caught Amara's eye, I knew she was feeling the same as I was. Calypso was gone. She was always so cryptic, but she was there when we needed her. I just hoped she would find peace with her sister wherever they were now.

Amara called out to those around us, "Esmeray should be weakened now, which means she will probably come for us to try and defeat us once and for all, and we need to be ready. We need to figure out how to return the gifts she had stolen back to their rightful Celestials."

The soldiers all nodded, looking ready for whatever Esmeray might throw their way. I could see the fear in some of their eyes, but they had fought alongside us this far, and they weren't about to give up now.

Amara turned to me, her eyes blazing with a fierce determination. "I think I may know a way to return their powers to them."

I nodded, waiting for her to continue. She pulled me aside and pulled a book out of her bag to show me.

"This is a book of spells Esmeray stole and used to take their powers; there must be a way that shows how to return them as well."

My eyes widened as I recognized the book. "A grimoire?"

"Yes."

I peered at the pages, trying to decipher the ancient text. "Can you read this?"

Amara nodded, her fingers tracing the words. "I don't know how, but yes."

My heart raced as she handed me the book, pointing to the spell in question. I read it over a few times, trying to commit it to memory.

"We'll need to gather the Celestials, and quickly," I said, handing the book back to her.

I watched as she walked over to the group of prisoners she and Wesley had rescued.

Xander made his way towards me, concern etched on his face. "Are you alright?"

I nodded, still trying to process everything that had happened. "Calypso sacrificed herself to weaken Esmeray. We've finally brought down the barrier, but now we need to return the stolen powers back to the Celestials and stop her once and for all."

Xander's expression hardened. "We'll do what we have to do. And we'll make sure Esmeray pays for what she's done."

Xander and I joined Amara, where she stood with most of the prisoners. Together, Amara, Xander, and I worked to gather the rest of the Celestials. The spell in the grimoire was intricate, and we needed everyone's powers to make it work.

A tall man with black, shoulder-length hair joined us, carrying over a heavy chest. He placed it on the ground next to us with a grunt.

"Thanks, Bastian," Amara said as she leaned down to open the chest. "Your powers and abilities are inside these crystals. We need to figure out whose is whose, and everyone needs to be holding the crystal containing their gift for it to be returned."

Bastian nodded, his piercing blue eyes scanning the crystals within the chest. "I'll help sort them out."

The air around us hummed with energy as the Celestials closed in. Bastian stepped forward and handed a crystal to a small woman whose red hair matched the intensity of the glowing gem. As soon as she touched it, its light increased exponentially, casting an eerie shine on all our faces.

I watched in awe as the crystals began to glow with a brilliant light. They hovered in the air, each one emitting a different aura. The Celestials stepped forward, each one taking hold of the crystal containing their gift.

Closing my eyes, focusing on the spell in the grimoire. I recited the words under my breath, pouring every bit of magic I had into it.

The air around us began to crackle with energy, and I felt a sense of power surge through me as the spell took hold. The crystals in their hands began to glow brighter and brighter, until they were almost blinding.

Suddenly, with a bright flash of light, the crystals shattered, and their gifts surged back into the Celestials. I watched in amazement as they were enveloped in the energy of their returned gifts, their eyes glowing with happiness and relief.

One by one, they stepped forward, thanking us with tears in their eyes. We had given them back what was rightfully theirs, and I knew that they would be stronger than ever.

Amara turned to me, her eyes shining with pride. "We did it."

I grinned back at her, feeling a sense of accomplishment like I had never felt before. We were one step closer to defeating Esmeray.

The cheers of the Celestials echoed through the once-shadowed landscape as their powers were restored. The air crackled with a newfound energy, and the sun bathed the land in a warm glow. We had achieved a small victory, but the looming threat of Esmeray still hung heavily over us.

Amara's gaze was unwavering as she addressed the gathered Celestials. "Now that your powers are returned, we need to prepare for Esmeray's retaliation. She won't take this lightly, and we must be ready for whatever she throws our way."

The Celestials nodded in understanding, their expressions resolute. The atmosphere had shifted from celebration to anticipation, and a steely determination settled over our makeshift army.

Xander approached me, his eyes reflecting the weight of the challenges ahead. "We need to fortify our defences and be vigilant. Esmeray is wounded, but she's still dangerous."

I nodded, the reality of the situation sinking in. "We should gather intelligence on her movements and plans. If we know what she's up to, we can strategize better."

Xander's eyes gleamed with what looked like pride. "I'll send scouts to keep an eye on the surrounding areas. We need to be one step ahead of her. And we shouldn't expect to leave the Shadow Lands until she is defeated."

I shivered at the thought of being trapped in this dark and dangerous place for any longer, but I knew that we had no other choice. The barrier was down, but who knew what still lurked around us? But we would do whatever it takes to stop Esmeray from causing any more harm.

As Xander went off to organize the scouts, I felt a hand on my shoulder. I turned to see Amara, her eyes filled with concern.

"Are you okay?" she asked softly.

I nodded, trying to hide the fear and uncertainty that were building inside me. "I'm fine. We just have a lot of work to do."

Amara gave me a small smile. "We can do this. We've come too far to give up now. And we have each other."

Her words were a comfort, and I felt a sense of camaraderie with her that I had never felt before. We were all in this together, fighting for a common cause, and I'd never felt closer.

Amara and I made our way to a quieter corner of the camp, away from the celebratory cheers and the strategic discussions. The night air was crisp, and a gentle breeze rustled the leaves above us. We both took a moment to catch our breath and process the whirlwind of events.

"I can't believe we actually did it," I said, my voice filled with a mixture of awe and disbelief. "The barrier is down, and the Celestials have their powers back."

Amara nodded, her eyes reflecting the same mix of emotions. "It's a significant victory, Avery. But we can't let our guard down. Esmeray will strike back, and we need to be ready."

The gravity of her words settled over us, a reminder that our journey was far from over. Despite the warmth of success, the shadow of impending danger lingered.

"Amara, I... I never imagined I'd be a part of something like this," I admitted, my gaze fixed on the distant horizon. "I was raised in the mortal world, not knowing anything about my true identity. And now, here I am, fighting alongside you for a cause that is so much bigger than myself."

Amara's expression softened, a sisterly understanding in her eyes. "I never knew you existed until recently. It's been a lot to take in, but having you by my side, fighting for our home, it means more to me than I can express."

I smiled, feeling a sense of connection that surpassed the blood ties we had only recently discovered. "We make a good team, don't we?"

She chuckled, the sound carrying a mix of fondness and sisterly affection. "We do. And I'm grateful for that. But there's so much more I want to know about you, Avery. About the life you led in the mortal world, about the person you were before all of this."

I sighed, realizing there was still so much we didn't know about each other. "I was raised in a small town; we didn't have a lot, but I had my adoptive mother. She's really the only thing I miss about my life back there. I went to see her before we came here. And I hope I'll get to see her again. I had no idea I had a twin sister or that I belonged to a world of magic and celestial beings."

Amara listened intently, her expression one of understanding. "I can only imagine how overwhelming all of this must be for you," she said softly. "But I want you to know that you have a place with us, Avery. You belong here with me, with all of us. And I promise you, we will do everything in our power to defeat Esmeray and keep Caelestia safe."

Her words filled me with a sense of comfort, and I knew that I had found a family here, one that I never knew I had. "Thank you, Amara. I'm grateful to have you as my sister."

She pulled me in for a brief hug, and as we parted, a sense of newfound closeness lingered between us. The camp buzzed with activity, but in that quiet moment, Amara and I forged a connection that surpassed the challenges ahead. We were sisters, united by blood and a shared destiny, ready to face whatever came our way.

CHAPTER TWENTY-ONE

Amara

Making my way through the bustling camp, the remnants of celebration still lingering in the air. My thoughts swirled with the weight of the recent small victory. Beneath it all, concern for Wesley tugged at me. As much as he tried to hide it and push through it all while we were in the midst of everything that had happened, I knew he was haunted by what he had done to me and the pain and torment he had inflicted on me. I had no idea what Esmeray had done to him after I left him in the Shadow Lands. But it had to be bad to have changed him so much.

I found Wesley sitting alone on the edge of the camp, his gaze fixed on the distant shadows that clung to the outskirts. The night air whispered through the trees, carrying a quiet sorrow that matched the gravity of our shared history.

Approaching him, I hesitated for a moment before sitting beside him. "Wesley," I began, my voice gentle, "how are you holding up?"

He glanced at me, his eyes reflecting a storm of emotions. "I've been better," he admitted, the weight of guilt evident in his words.

I nodded, understanding the internal struggle he faced. "I know it must be hard for you, especially after everything Esmeray must have done to you."

Wesley sighed, his gaze dropping to the ground. "It's more than that, Amara. Before you came back, before any of this, I was stuck in the Shadow Lands for what felt like years. Time moved differently there, faster than it did in Caelestia."

My brows furrowed in concern. "So how long exactly were you there for?" I knew he mentioned this before when I was his prisoner; he had said something about me leaving him there for years.

"About two years," he replied, the weight of each word hanging in the air.

My eyes widened, realizing the extent of the suffering he had endured. "Two years? Wesley, I had no idea. When you pushed me through the barrier—when I returned to Soluna—it was as if no time had passed. I thought I had more time to come back to save you. I wanted to save you." I choked back the tears that wanted to fall.

Pain etched into the lines of his face. "I know. It doesn't matter now. But at that time, Esmeray tortured me, twisted my mind. She made me hate everything and everyone, especially you."

Guilt kneaded at my chest. "I'm so sorry you had to go through all of that."

He looked at me, his gaze softened by a mixture of pain and understanding. "I know that now. But back then, I couldn't see past the darkness she wrapped around me. She gave me dark magic, Amara. I can wield shadows because I became a faithful follower of hers."

"You were trapped, manipulated. None of this is your fault."

Wesley nodded, a weary acceptance in his eyes. "I know that. But it doesn't change what I did to you. I hurt you, and I can't erase that."

I placed a comforting hand on his shoulder. "We all have scars, Wesley. What matters now is how we move forward. We're in this together, fighting against Esmeray. You've shown that you can resist her influence."

A flicker of gratitude passed through his eyes. "Thanks, Amara. I just... I needed you to know the truth. About everything."

I took a deep breath, weighed down by the gravity of the situation. "Thank you for telling me, Wesley. It takes courage to face the past, even the painful parts. But we're in this together, and I won't let you face it alone."

He gave me a small, grateful smile, and for a moment, the weight of our shared history felt a little lighter. "I'm glad you're here, Amara," he said quietly. "I don't know where I'd be without you."

A sense of warmth blossomed in my chest, and I leaned in to give him a hug. "You're not alone, Wesley. We'll get through this together."

As we parted, the weight of the impending battle hung heavy in the air. But there was a sense of hope too, a reminder that even in the midst of darkness, there was always light to be found. Together, we would face whatever came our way, united in our bond and our resolve to protect Caelestia from Esmeray's grasp.

CHAPTER TWENTY-TWO

Avery

With so many people dispersed with the preparations, Xander and I found a moment of quiet amidst the bustling activity. The weight of the upcoming battle lingered in the air, but for now, we were free to steal a moment away.

Xander took my hand, leading me away from the group. We walked in silence for a while, the quiet surroundings making it easier for me to gather my thoughts. I knew that this would be the calm before the storm, and I tried to make the most of it.

His eyes softened as he looked at me. "We've been through so much in such a short amount of time, haven't we?"

I just nodded in response.

"Are you scared?" he asked gently.

Turning to him, my eyes betraying the fear that I had tried to keep hidden. "A little," I admitted.

Understanding etched in his expression, he said, "We'll get through this together. And I promise you, I won't let anything happen to you."

I smiled at him, taking comfort in his words. "I know. And I won't let anything happen to you either."

His hand reached up to cup my cheek. "I'm proud of you, Avery. You've shown incredible strength and leadership."

I leaned into his touch, feeling a warmth spread through me. "I couldn't have done it without you."

He smiled, his thumb tracing my cheekbone. "We make a good team."

We stood in silence for a moment, the gravity of our situation weighing heavy on us. But then Xander leaned in, his lips meeting mine in a soft, tender kiss. It was a brief respite from the chaos around us, and I savoured every moment of it.

Pulling away, Xander looked at me with a hint of mischief in his eyes. "You know, we could always sneak away and hide from all this," he whispered.

I chuckled, feeling a lightness in my chest that I hadn't felt in a while. "And where would we go?"

He grinned, pulling me closer. "Anywhere. As long as I'm with you, I don't care where we are."

I wrapped my arms around his neck, lost in the moment.

"Oh really?" I teased.

"I love you," he breathed out with a deeper intensity as his gaze held mine.

My heart swelled with emotion as I replied, "I love you too."

Xander's lips found mine again, and this time the kiss was more urgent, more demanding. Our bodies pressed together, the heat between us igniting a fire that threatened to consume us both. It was as if we were the only two people in the world, and nothing else mattered except this moment.

But soon, the reality of the situation we were in hit me. We couldn't hide away, not when there was so much at stake.

I pulled back from Xander, my expression serious. "We can't run away from this, Xander. We have to face it head-on."

He nodded in agreement. "I know."

"Avery! Xander! Come quickly!" It was Amara's voice, urgent and panicked.

We looked at one another before breaking back and dashing back towards the group. As we neared the source of the disturbance, we saw that a group of scouts had returned with worrying news.

"She's coming," one of them panted out. "Esmeray is on her way."

The atmosphere shifted from anticipation to fear, and I could feel my heart rate increasing. We had known that this moment would come, but the reality of it all was still overwhelming.

"We need to prepare," Amara said firmly, her voice shaking slightly. "Get everyone to their positions, and make sure the defences are sturdy."

Xander nodded in agreement, his jaw set in determination. "We'll fight her with everything we've got."

I squared my shoulders, ready to face whatever was coming our way. We had come too far to back down now. The fate of Soluna—and all of Caelestia—depended on us, and I was ready to fight for it.

But as we made our way to our designated positions, a sense of fear crept up on me. What if I wasn't strong enough? What if we were not prepared for what was coming?

As the battleground took shape, I stood alongside Xander, Amara, and the other Celestials. In the distance, Esmeray marched towards us, shrouded in darkness and emitting a palpable air of evil. The very atmosphere around her seemed to be afflicted by her presence.

Without hesitation, she unleashed her power, sending dark tendrils of energy toward us. The clash of magic and the deafening sounds of combat echoed through the Shadow Lands.

Xander and I moved in unison, with him drawing his sword and me summoning the water within me. But this time, something felt different. A surge of power coursed through my veins, and a sense of familiarity washed over me.

I called upon my water nymphs, and for the first time in what felt like an eternity, they answered. From the shadows, ethereal figures emerged, shimmering in the darkness. They were *my* warriors, made of water, graceful, and deadly.

With newfound strength and confidence, I directed the water nymphs to engage the dark forces unleashed by Esmeray. They moved with an otherworldly grace, slicing through the dark tendrils with ease. It was as if they danced on the edge of reality, a manifestation of the water's essence.

Beside me, Amara conjured flames that danced in rhythm with the water nymphs. The battlefield became a symphony of elements, a clash between light and shadow.

Xander, Erik, Victoria, Larina, and Lieutenant-General McKenna, alongside countless unnamed soldiers, engaged the demons with unyielding resolve. Their skill in combat was our shield against Esmeray's relentless assault.

I watched as Xander battled fiercely, his sword glinting in the darkness. He moved with a fluidity that was almost mesmerizing, his movements a deadly dance. His eyes met mine for a moment, and I could see the determination and love in them.

It was that love that drove me forward.

The battle raged on, the ground shaking with every blow. Blood and sweat mingled in the air, the scent of fear and desperation overwhelming. I lost sight of my friends and family around me. But despite the chaos, I remained focused, my mind clear and steady.

Esmeray was strong, but so were we.

Summoning all the water within me, I channelled it into a powerful wave that crashed against Esmeray. The impact sent her flying back, and for a moment, it seemed like we had won.

But then the darkness around her swirled, and she rose again, her eyes blazing with an intensity that made my blood run cold. She was more powerful than we had anticipated, and she was not going to be defeated so easily.

Esmeray unleashed a barrage of dark magic, and I felt my strength waning. I tried to summon more water, but I could feel myself growing weaker by the second. It was as if my body was being drained of all its energy.

I looked around, seeing my friends and comrades faltering under the onslaught of Esmeray's power. Their faces were twisted in agony, their movements slow and sluggish. I knew then that we were in trouble. We had underestimated our enemy, and now we were paying the price.

The sky suddenly darkened, and a loud rumble echoed in the air. Lightning flashed and forked down on the earth like swords slashing out of the sky. An army of demons descending from the clouds, their wings beating furiously as they flew towards us.

Outnumbered and outmatched, our forces fought valiantly despite overwhelming odds. But it soon became clear that this was no ordinary enemy we faced; these creatures moved like shadows in the night, striking without warning or mercy.

Amara stepped forward then, her hands glowing with power as she summoned a wall of flames between us and our foes. The fire blazed brightly against the darkness, burning away at everything in its path. For a moment, it seemed like we might prevail against this new onslaught, but then a figure appeared from the flames, shrouded in a cloak of darkness that seemed to be alive.

Esmeray.

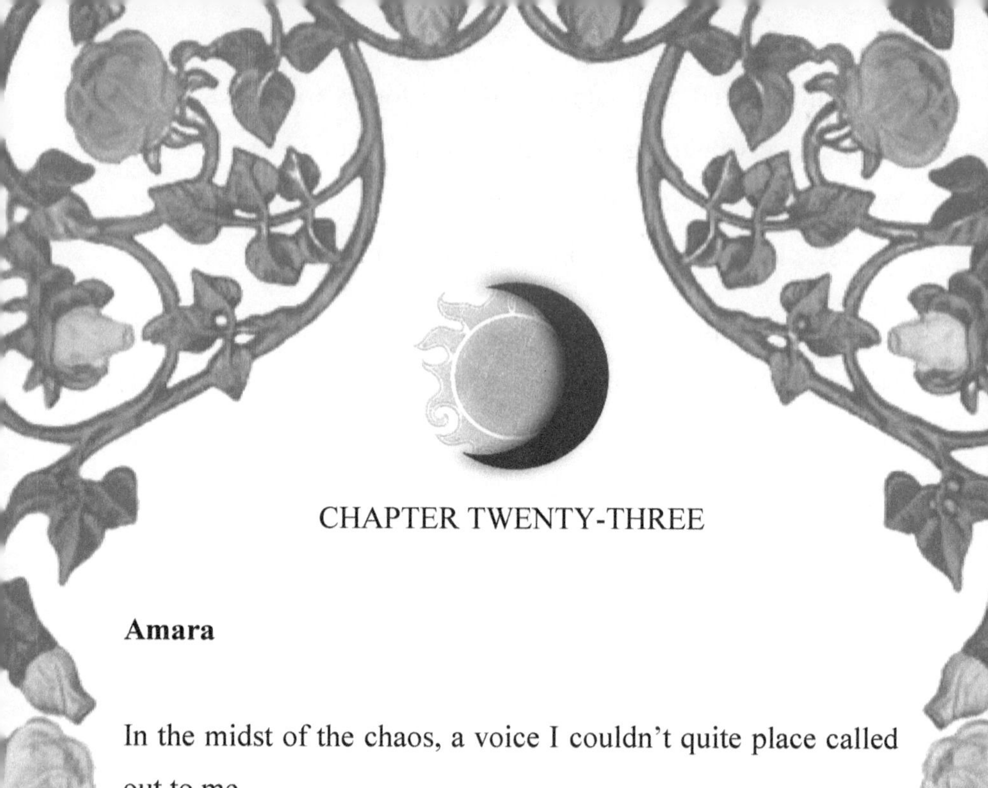

CHAPTER TWENTY-THREE

Amara

In the midst of the chaos, a voice I couldn't quite place called out to me.

"Amara!"

I spun around and scanned the trees through squinted eyes. There, at the edge of the clearing, stood some familiar faces. They waved and shouted as they sprinted towards me.

"Orion!" I called, running up to meet them. "I wasn't sure if you survived or if you had joined Esmeray's side."

His eyes crinkled as he forced a tight smile. "It was hard once we found out Ophiuchus had been working for the Shadow Lord the entire time, but we fought back, and we're here to help you fight again."

"Thank the gods," I breathed out, pulling them into a tight embrace. "We need all the help we can get."

Orion's expression turned serious. "What's the plan?"

Wesley joined us, the two nodding at one another. "We need to defeat Esmeray. We've weakened her, but she is still incredibly powerful."

I nodded, scanning the battlefield. Our forces were starting to falter, and Esmeray was still standing. It was clear that we needed to do something drastic.

"We need a distraction," I said, my mind racing. "Something to draw her attention away from us."

Orion cocked his head, considering. "I might know someone who can help with that."

"Who?" I asked eagerly.

He hesitated for a moment before answering. "My brother. He's a shapeshifter. He can take on any form, and he's always looking for a good fight."

I raised an eyebrow. "Sounds like just the distraction we need. Do you think he'll be willing to help us?"

Orion grinned. "Oh, he'll be more than willing. He's been itching for a good battle for months now."

I couldn't help but smile at his enthusiasm. "Great. Let's go find him."

We made our way through the battlefield, ducking and weaving as we dodged blasts of magic and demonic strikes.

Finally, we reached the centre of the fight, calling out to his brother to get his attention just as he lopped off a demon's head. I conjured a ring of flames around us to keep the demons at bay while we went over this new plan.

"Bash!"

"You've got to be kidding me," I muttered just as Bastian turned around. He wore a wicked grin as he spotted us.

"You're brothers?" Wesley asked, his brows furrowed together.

"Yeah," they said in unison as Bastian patted Orion on the shoulder.

"And you can shapeshift?" I blurted. "Why didn't you tell me that when you got your powers back?"

"You never asked," he shrugged. "I mean, you really should have figured out what each of our powers were to see how we could use them in this war."

"Yeah, yeah. We don't really have time for this." I cut in, my patience wearing thin. "Esmeray is still out there, and we need your help."

Bastian's expression turned serious. "What do you need me to do?"

"We need a distraction," I explained, laying out our plan. "We need you to take on a form that will draw Esmeray's attention away from us."

Bastian grinned, rubbing his hands together. "I've got just the thing."

Orion stepped forward, clasping his brother's shoulder. "Be careful, Bash. Esmeray is powerful. Don't underestimate her."

Bastian's grin faltered for a moment, but then he straightened. "I won't. You guys take care of yourselves."

Dropping my fire wall, we returned to the battle at hand. But just as Bastian was about to leave, the sky darkened around us, and more and more demons descended from the skies.

I called upon my flames once more to fight against the demons. Wesley fought by my side, wielding his own shadow magic against them. The scars of his past lingered, but the fire of determination burned brightly in his eyes.

Orion darted around the battlefield, his sword flashing as he cut down demons left and right. But despite our best efforts, the demons just kept coming, and it wasn't long before they had us surrounded.

I summoned a curtain of flames, pulsing and roiling in darkness, stretching out to form an impenetrable barrier between us and the approaching demons. Esmeray stepped through my fire unharmed, as if its scorching heat could not touch her, responding to my efforts with a stoic silence. Her silhouette seemed to be shrouded in a cloak of shadows that only seemed to amplify her strength.

Just when it seemed like we were doomed, a deafening roar echoed across the battlefield, shaking the very ground beneath our feet. We looked up, and there, hovering above us, was Bastian.

But it wasn't the familiar form of his human self that we saw. Instead, he had transformed into a giant golden dragon.

Esmeray's attention was immediately drawn to the dragon. She unleashed a barrage of dark magic at it, but Bastian breathed fire and lightning towards her magic. The battlefield was bathed in the glow of the dragon's power.

"Shine your light and illuminate the world," A voice sang in my mind.

Calypso. Her name echoed in my mind, stirring up a flurry of bittersweet emotions. But I was so grateful that she had sacrificed herself to give us a fighting chance. I wished I could have done more to help her, but now all I could do was remember her and everything she'd told us.

Then it came to me: I needed to find Avery. We needed to defeat Esmeray *together*.

I turned to Wesley, grabbing his arm. "Wesley, we need to find Avery. She might be our only chance to defeat Esmeray."

He nodded. "Let's go."

We darted through the battlefield, avoiding demons and dodging blasts of dark magic. Finally, we saw a group of warriors surrounding Avery in the distance. They were fighting fiercely against the demons, but they were slowly being pushed back.

"Avery!" I screamed, catching her attention. "We need your help!"

She turned towards us, her eyes widening in surprise. "Amara, what's going on?"

"We need you to help us defeat Esmeray," I explained quickly. "Bastian is distracting her now, but we need to finish her off."

Avery nodded, resolve burning brightly in her eyes. "Let's go."

Together, we ran towards Esmeray—the Shadow Lord. She was still battling Bastian, but she turned her attention towards us as we approached. Her eyes glinted with malice as she prepared to unleash her dark magic upon us.

But Avery was ready. She raised her hands, calling upon her own magic. The two forces collided, and for a moment, it seemed like the entire world was bathed in darkness.

Then, a brilliant silver light erupted from Avery's hands, pushing back against the darkness. The light grew brighter and brighter, until it was blinding.

Esmeray growled in frustration, but before she could regroup, Wesley leaped forward, his shadow magic wrapping around her limbs and holding her in place.

I stepped forward, placing my hand in Avery's, and together we channelled our magic into the blinding light. The light intensified, enveloping us all in a warm, comforting embrace. Esmeray screamed in agony as the light consumed her. The light faded away, and she was gone.

The darkness that had shrouded the battlefield lifted, and the demons that had been fighting against us vanished into thin air. We stood there for a moment, panting and covered in sweat and grime, but triumphant.

"We did it," Avery breathed, a smile spreading across her face.

"Yeah," Wesley agreed, a look of relief and exhaustion washing over his features.

Xander stepped forward, his eyes shining with pride. "You guys are amazing," he said as he pulled Avery into a tight embrace.

I smiled, feeling a warm sense of satisfaction spreading through my body. "We couldn't have done it without all of you," I said, looking around at my friends and newfound allies.

As we celebrated our victory, I felt a hand slip into mine. I turned to see Wesley, his eyes filled with an emotion that I couldn't quite place.

"Thank you," he said, his voice barely above a whisper. "For coming back to me."

I squeezed his hand. "Of course. That's what friends are for."

"Friends," he repeated, a small smile tugging at his lips.

I looked around at my friends, seeing the relief and exhaustion etched on their faces. We had been through so much together, and now we could finally rest.

But as I glanced back over at Wesley, I noticed a flicker of something in his eyes. "I'm sorry," he breathed.

"For what?"

"For what I did to you when I wasn't myself," he said, his voice heavy with regret.

I looked at him, my heart aching for him. "Wesley, it wasn't your fault. You don't need to keep apologizing to me for when you were under Esmeray's control."

"I know," he said, "but I... I just—"

I stepped closer to him, reaching up to touch his cheek. "Wesley, you're here now. That's all that matters."

His eyes locked onto mine, and in that moment, I knew that we had both survived the war, but we were left with scars that would never fully heal.

But together, we could face anything.

As the sun began to set over the battlefield, we gathered around a small fire, sharing stories and memories of those we had lost. The air was filled with a mix of laughter and tears as we reminisced about the good times we had shared with our fallen comrades.

Wesley's hand slipped into mine, and I turned to him, a small smile gracing my lips. He returned the smile, and we sat there in contented silence, taking comfort in each other's presence.

As the night wore on, our group began to disperse, each of us finding our own place to rest and recover. Wesley and I found a spot near the fire, settling in for the night.

As we lay there, wrapped in each other's arms, I couldn't help but feel a sense of peace wash over me. For the first time in a long time, I felt safe.

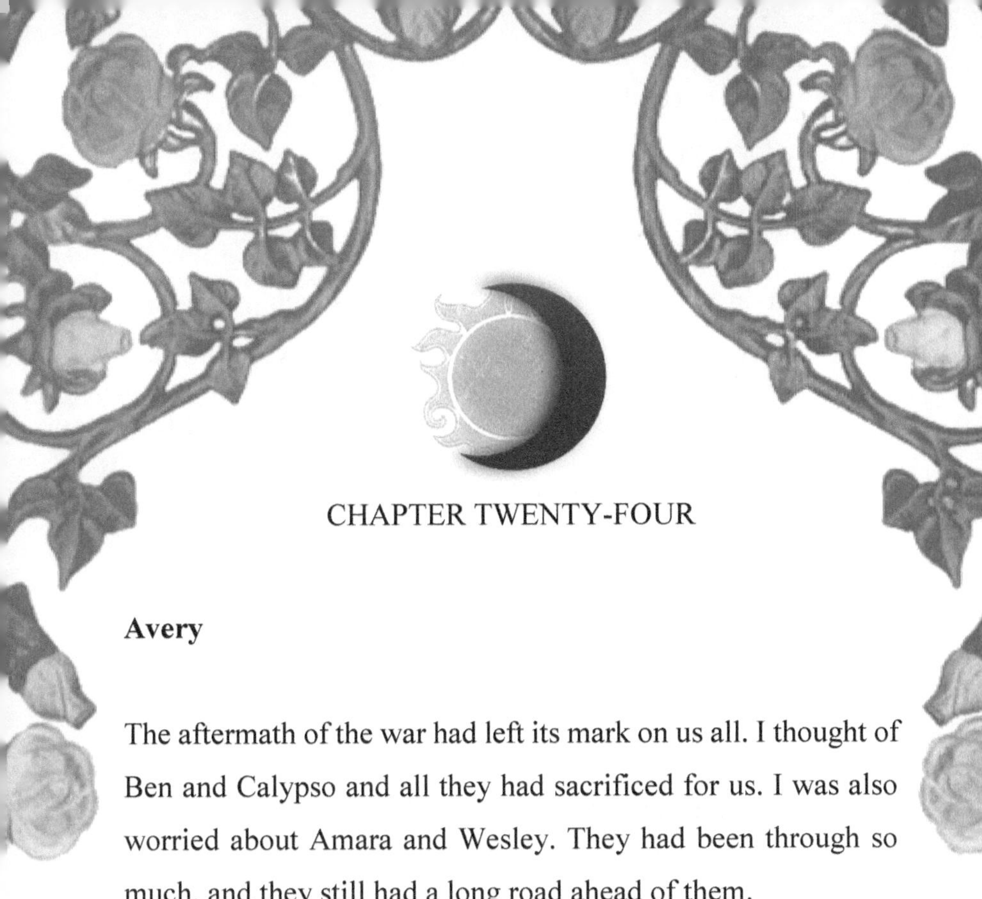

CHAPTER TWENTY-FOUR

Avery

The aftermath of the war had left its mark on us all. I thought of Ben and Calypso and all they had sacrificed for us. I was also worried about Amara and Wesley. They had been through so much, and they still had a long road ahead of them.

I watched them from a distance, their bodies entwined together as they sat alone near the fire. Their faces were peaceful, but I knew that their minds were likely filled with memories of their time trapped inside the Shadow Lands. I sighed, knowing that there was nothing I could do to ease their pain.

Suddenly, I felt a hand on my shoulder. I turned to see Xander standing there, his expression sombre.

"Hey," he said softly. "How are you holding up?"

I shrugged, not really sure how to answer. "I'm okay, I guess. It's just a lot to process."

He nodded. "Yeah, I know what you mean."

We sat in silence for a few moments, watching the fire crackle and pop. Then Xander turned to me, his eyes serious.

"I wanted to talk to you about something," he said slowly.

"Okay," I replied, suddenly feeling a sense of unease.

"I know we've been through a lot together," he began, "and I know that we've both lost people we care about. But I also know that life is short, and we never know when our time will be up."

I frowned, not sure where he was going with this. "What are you trying to say, Xander?"

"About what we said earlier..." he trailed off.

Oh god, please don't tell me he regrets it, didn't mean it, or it was just a heat of the moment thing.

"I just wanted to make sure that you knew that I meant it," he continued, his voice softening. "I care about you, Avery. A lot."

I felt my heart skip a beat, and a small smile tugged at the corners of my lips. "I care about you too, Xander," I said, reaching out to take his hand.

He squeezed my hand, his eyes filled with a mix of emotions. "Good," he murmured, leaning in to press his lips gently against mine.

As we kissed, I felt a sense of rightness settle over me. Despite all that we had been through, we had still managed to find love in the midst of chaos.

As we pulled away, Xander rested his forehead against mine, his eyes closed. "I don't want to lose you," he murmured, his voice barely above a whisper.

"You won't," I promised, wrapping my arms around him.

Xander pulled back slightly, his eyes searching mine. "Are you sure?" he asked, his voice tinged with worry.

I nodded, knowing that my heart had already made its decision. "I'm sure," I said softly. "I want to be with you."

Relief flooded his features, and he pulled me into another embrace. "I'm so glad," he murmured into my hair.

Xander held me tightly, and for a moment, all of the worries and fears that had been weighing on me melted away. I could feel his warmth and strength, and it filled me with a sense of hope for the future.

We sat there for a while longer, watching the stars twinkle above us. We talked about everything and nothing, enjoying each other's company and the peace that came with it.

Eventually, we both began to feel the exhaustion of the day catch up to us. We stood up, brushing the dirt and debris off our clothes. Xander took my hand, leading me towards a small tent that had been set up for us.

But as the night wore on, I found myself unable to sleep. Memories of the war and the people we had lost kept swirling around in my head, and I couldn't shake the feeling that our victory had come at too high a cost.

I slipped out of Xander's embrace, careful not to wake him, and made my way over to the edge of the campsite. The air was cool and crisp, and the stars shone brightly in the sky.

As I stared up at the stars, lost in thought, I heard footsteps behind me. "Couldn't sleep either?" Amara's voice was soft, and I turned to see her standing there, her eyes filled with sympathy.

I shook my head. "No. Too much on my mind." She nodded, understanding written on her face. "I know what you mean. It's hard to forget what we've been through."

We stood there in silence for a few moments, both lost in our own thoughts.

"So... what happens now?" I asked, breaking the silence.

"What do you want to happen next?" A small smile pulled at her lips.

I glanced back at the tent where Xander was still sleeping.

"After everything that's happened, I don't know if I want to go back to my world."

Amara's expression softened as she stepped closer to me. "You don't have to," she said, her voice low. "You can stay here, with us."

I nodded, feeling the weight of the decision settle over me. "I mean, I don't know what I would go back to other than my mom. My life was pretty…ordinary before all of this."

"And now?" Amara prompted.

"Now, I feel like I've been a part of something bigger than myself," I said, my voice strong. "I've seen things that I never would have thought possible, and I've been a part of a team that faced the impossible and came out victorious."

Amara smiled at me, her eyes shining with pride. "You have," she said. "And you've proven yourself to be one of the strongest and bravest people I've ever met."

"Thank you," I said softly.

"Of course," she replied. "And just remember, whatever you decide, we'll be here for you."

I smiled, feeling a sense of comfort in her words. "Thank you," I said again.

As we stood there, the sound of footsteps caught our attention, and we turned to see Xander approaching us.

"Hey," he said, his voice hoarse. "What are you guys doing out here?"

"Just talking," Amara replied, a small smile on her lips.

Xander nodded, but I could tell that he was still half asleep. "Well, it's freezing out here," he murmured, wrapping an arm around my waist and pulling me close. "Let's head back to the tent."

Amara nodded, and we all walked back to the tents. As Xander and I crawled back into the tent we shared, I felt a sense of peace settle over me. No matter what the future held, I knew that I had people who cared about me and a place where I belonged.

As I drifted off to sleep, I couldn't help but feel grateful for the bond that had been forged between us after everything we'd been through since I arrived.

The next morning, we began to pack up our campsite. The air was crisp, and the sky was clear. The sun was just beginning to rise, and it was time to journey back to Soluna. It was much easier with the Celestials' power restored and the curse preventing everyone from remembering magic lifted.

As we walked, I couldn't help but notice the way Xander kept stealing glances at me. I smiled, feeling my cheeks heat up. It was still so new, this thing between us, but it felt right.

We walked in silence for a while, lost in our own thoughts. But eventually, Xander took my hand, giving it a gentle squeeze. "Are you okay?" he asked softly.

I nodded, feeling a sense of warmth spread through me at the touch of his hand. "Yeah, I'm good. Just...thinking," I replied.

"About what?" he prompted.

I hesitated for a moment, unsure if I was ready to share my innermost thoughts with him just yet. But then I took a deep breath, steeling my resolve. "About what comes next," I said, my voice low.

Xander looked at me, his eyes filled with a mix of understanding and concern. "You know you don't have to decide anything right away, right?" he said, his thumb tracing circles on the back of my hand.

"I know," I replied. "It's just...I don't know what I want to do. Stay here, go back to my world...it's all so confusing."

"It's okay," Xander said, his voice soft. "Just take your time. We'll figure it out together."

I smiled at him, feeling a sense of gratitude wash over me. "Thank you," I said.

We walked on, our hands still intertwined. I thought about what Amara had said to me the night before. About staying here with them. It was tempting. I had found a sense of purpose and belonging here that I had never felt before.

But at the same time, I knew that I couldn't stay. I had a life back home, and what about my mom?

Xander must have sensed the turmoil inside me because he stopped walking and turned to face me. "Talk to me," he said gently. "What's on your mind?"

Sighing, I felt the weight of the decision settle over me. "I want to stay," I said quietly. "But I can't abandon my mom."

"I understand," Xander said, his voice soft. "But that doesn't mean you have to leave everything behind. Maybe there's a way for you to balance both worlds."

I looked at him, feeling a sense of hope stirring within me. "What do you mean?"

"I mean, maybe you can find a way to visit your world while still being a part of ours," he said, his eyes bright. "I mean, you have literal magic; I'm sure you can make it work."

I couldn't help but smile at his words, feeling a sense of relief wash over me. He was right. I had magic. I could find a way to balance both worlds.

"That's a great idea," I said, feeling my spirits lift. "I could visit my mom and then come back here."

"Exactly," Xander said, his eyes shining with excitement. "And who knows, maybe you could even bring her here someday."

"Yeah, maybe." I laughed while squeezing his hand, feeling a sense of comfort in his touch. "Thank you," I said softly.

"Of course," he replied, his thumb still tracing circles on the back of my hand. "I want you to be happy, wherever you are."

"I am," I said, looking up at him. "With you, Amara, and everyone. I am happy."

Xander's face broke into a wide grin before he leaned down and pressed his lips to mine. It was a gentle kiss, filled with all the tenderness and love that we had for each other. When we pulled away, we both had goofy grins on our faces.

"Come on," he said, tugging on my hand. "Let's catch up with the others."

We started walking again, and the sun was now fully up. We caught up with Amara and the rest of the group. They were all laughing and chatting, but as soon as they saw us, they fell quiet. I could feel their eyes on us, and I blushed, feeling self-conscious.

But then Hazel spoke up, her voice warm. "Glad to see you two are getting along," she said, a sly grin on her face.

I laughed, feeling a sense of ease settle over me. Maybe things were going to be okay after all.

It was a long journey back to Estrella and the castle, but it was a journey filled with hope. I knew that whatever came next, I had a support system of people who loved and cared for me.

And with Xander by my side, I felt like I could conquer anything.

The castle rose before us, its massive towers and stone walls looming over the road. I was mesmerized. The setting sun cast a deep golden glow on the entire structure, illuminating the turrets and ivy-covered walls. It was even more beautiful than I remembered. This was my home now, and I was ready to embrace it.

Xander squeezed my hand. "Ready?" he asked softly.

I nodded, anticipation building inside me. We walked through the gates, and a sense of familiarity washed over me. This was my world now, and I was ready for it.

We slowly made our way through the castle courtyard, heads held high and arms linked. Guards and servants stepped aside to bow in recognition, but their eyes were wide with curiosity as they noticed both me and Amara.

As we continued on our way, an overwhelming sense of pride swelled within me as we walked through the halls that were so familiar to me now. This was where I belonged.

But as we approached the throne room, a sudden commotion caught our attention. We quickened our pace and entered the room to find a group of people gathered inside. It was the council, and they looked like they were in the middle of a heated discussion. I couldn't help but feel a sense of unease as we approached, wondering if they were discussing something important. The sound of their arguments filled the room. It was clear that something was amiss.

I looked to Amara, who had a similar expression of concern on her face. We made our way through the group until we stood in front of the council.

Their eyes widened as they took us both in.

"Your Highness," one of the council members said, bowing low as his gaze darted between the two of us.

The council members exchanged glances, clearly unsure about my presence in the throne room.

Amara stepped forward, her voice ringing out clear and authoritative. "Council members, I present to you Princess Avery, my twin sister and rightful co-heir to the throne of Soluna."

The room fell silent, and I felt a deep sense of apprehension settle over me. This was it. The moment of truth.

The council members exchanged uneasy glances once more, their expressions filled with uncertainty. I could tell that they were struggling to come to terms with the revelation that there were two heirs to the throne. I stood beside Amara, feeling a sense of unease settle in my stomach. What would they say? What would they do?

Finally, one of the council members stepped forward, his expression grave and his voice hesitant. "Your Highness, we had no idea that you existed." They looked between the two of us, unable to deny that we were identical. "Which one of you is the rightful heir?"

"I think you misheard me, councilmen; we are co-heirs; we will both become queens," Amara responded firmly, her eyes locked with theirs. "We will rule together, as sisters and equals. It is what our father would have wanted."

The council members exchanged uneasy glances yet again, clearly unsure about this new development. But I could see that some of them were already beginning to see the wisdom in Amara's words.

The prophecy. I thought.

"The prophecy has always stated that there would be two rulers and they would bring the rise of two kingdoms; that is what we have done now that we have restored the Shadow Lands to what it once was." I grabbed Amara's hand in mine. "*We* are the true heirs."

There was a moment of tense silence as the council members processed our words. But then one of them stepped forward, her expression serious. "Your Highnesses, while this is certainly an unexpected turn of events, we will honour your wishes to rule together as co-heirs."

Murmurs of agreement rang from the other council members, and relief washed over me.

Lawrence stepped into the room, and as soon as his eyes landed on us, he smiled brightly—probably the biggest smile I'd ever seen on him, if I were being honest. I wanted to ask him about everything that we'd missed here while we were gone, but I knew it had to wait until the council was gone. I hoped he was no longer plagued by nightmares of his sister.

"Your Highnesses," Lawrence said proudly as he bowed to the both of us.

"You knew about this?" one of the councilmen asked.

Lawrence nodded. "It was always the King and Queen's dream for their daughters to rule together. Before the King and Queen had to send the princess away, they had entrusted me with the knowledge of their plan. I was sworn to secrecy and to watch over her for her safety until it was time for her to return home."

The council members shared skeptical looks as they weighed this new information in their minds. Some of the older members' faces lit up with recognition, as if the mention of this had helped break a spell that had been placed over them, and I was willing to bet that was exactly what had happened.

I looked to Lawrence, and he winked at me, practically confirming my suspicions. Calypso had given him a protection spell that had always kept his memories intact; it would make sense that the rest of the council *would* have known about me after my birth but had been spelled to forget me after I was sent away.

"I see," one of the council members said slowly. "Well, regardless, it seems that the prophecy has come to pass. Two rulers have indeed arisen, and two kingdoms have been united."

There was a sense of finality in his tone, and I could tell that the council had come to a decision. I felt a weight lifted off my shoulders, knowing that we finally had their support.

"Very well," another council member said, standing up from his seat. "We shall make the necessary arrangements for the coronation of our new co-heirs."

I felt a rush of excitement I hadn't really expected now that I was going to be crowned queen. I looked at Amara, and she smiled at me, her eyes filled with pride and affection.

"We did it," she whispered, her voice choked with emotion.

I smiled back at her, feeling a deep sense of gratitude and love wash over me.

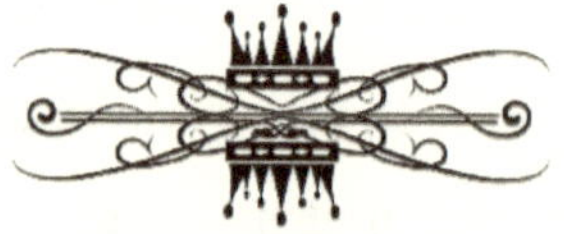

After the councillors left, we followed Lawrence back to his office. We wanted to properly fill him in on everything that had happened in the Shadow Lands, and we wanted to know what happened here while we were gone.

As soon as we were settled in Lawrence's office, Amara and I launched into the story of our journeys, describing everything from the demon attacks to having to sacrifice Calypso to Amara's time in the dungeons and freeing the other Celestials.

He listened intently, nodding and asking questions whenever he felt it was necessary. I could tell he was impressed by what we had accomplished, and it felt good to have someone acknowledge our hard work.

As we began to talk about what had happened in Soluna while we were gone, Lawrence's expression grew more serious. "Your Highnesses, it hasn't been easy," he said, pouring each of us a drink from his small table next to his desk. "The Duke of Caelia had yet again freed himself from the dungeons and managed to gain more support in your absences. But he has not been seen in a couple days now."

Amara and I exchanged worried looks. "What do you mean, he hasn't been seen?" I asked, feeling a sense of unease settle in my stomach.

Lawrence took a sip of his drink before continuing. "We don't know. There have been rumours that he may have fled the kingdom, but nothing has been confirmed."

"Fled?" Amara echoed, her voice filled with disbelief. "Why would he do that?"

"It's unclear," Lawrence replied, his brow furrowed in concern. "But the fact remains that he is no longer in Soluna."

"He was dead," I murmured, trying to piece everything together.

"Pardon?" Lawrence asked as his and Amara's gazes swung my way.

"We know that Esmeray killed him; I saw it happen. What if he is gone now because she was the only thing keeping him alive with her dark magic?"

Lawrence's eyes widened as the implications of my words sank in. "That's a possibility," he said slowly, his voice laced with concern.

If Chaz had indeed been kept alive by Esmeray's dark magic, then it was possible he was truly gone now that she had been defeated.

"We will have to keep an eye out for any signs of his return," Lawrence said, determination in his voice. "But for now, we need to focus on your coronation. It's only a few days away."

I nodded, grateful for the change of topic. The thought of becoming a queen still filled me with a sense of nervous excitement.

"We should also start thinking about what we want to accomplish as co-rulers," Amara said, a thoughtful expression on her face.

I nodded in agreement. The Shadow Lands had been our top priority, but now that we had restored them to their former glory and magic had returned to the lands of Caelestia, we needed to think about what we wanted to do next.

Lawrence smiled at us, pride evident in his eyes. "I have no doubt that the two of you will do great things for our kingdoms. Your mother and father would be proud."

The mention of our parents brought a pang of sadness to my heart, but I pushed it away. Now was not the time for grieving.

"We will make them proud," I said, resolve ringing in my voice.

CHAPTER TWENTY-FIVE

Amara

The next few days were a blur of preparations for our coronation. The entire palace had become a flurry of activity as the council and the servants worked tirelessly to ensure that everything was perfect. Dresses were fitted, flowers were arranged, and the palace was decorated to the nines.

Avery and I spent most of our time meeting with advisors, reviewing decrees, and finalizing the guest list for the coronation ceremony. I tried to sneak in as much time as I could to visit Wesley. I knew he was still struggling from his time trapped inside the Shadow Lands and what he had been forced to do to me.

It was a delicate balance between our duties as rulers and our personal lives. As much as we wanted to spend time with each other and with our loved ones, there was simply too much to do.

But in those rare moments of respite, Avery and I would sneak away to be with the men we loved. It was nice having a sister to share everything with. We talked about everything and nothing, enjoying the quiet moments we could steal away from the chaos of our impending coronation.

In the past, I had been so consumed by my responsibilities as future queen that I'd pushed away any chance at true happiness with the man I loved. But now, I was determined to make it work with Wesley; after all we'd been through together, we deserved a happily ever after.

Finally, the day of our coronation arrived, and I knew I needed to see him before the ceremony started. I slipped away from the bustling palace and made my way to the gardens, where I had asked him to meet me. As I entered the gardens, I saw him standing by the fountain, his eyes trained on the water as it cascaded down the tiers.

I walked up to him, feeling a sense of calm wash over me as he turned to face me. His eyes softened as they met mine, and I felt myself get lost in their depths.

"Hey," he said softly, his voice full of emotion.

"Hey," I replied, a small smile tugging at the corner of my lips.

We stood there in silence for a few moments, just enjoying each other's presence. It was as if the world around us had faded away, and it was just the two of us standing there.

Wesley reached out and took my hand, his touch sending shivers down my spine.

"I've missed you," he said, his voice barely above a whisper.

"I've missed you too," I replied, squeezing his hand.

He leaned in and kissed me, his lips soft and gentle against mine. It was like coming home, and I felt my body relax into his embrace.

"I wish we could stay here forever," he said, pulling away and looking into my eyes.

"Me too," I agreed, but I knew we couldn't. My responsibilities to the throne called, and we couldn't ignore them forever. "I don't know how I'm supposed to balance our relationship and my responsibilities. I just don't want to let you or the kingdom down."

Wesley's expression softened, and he pulled me into a tight embrace. "You won't let anyone down," he said firmly. "I know how important your duties are, but you're also allowed to have a life outside of them. We can make it work, Amara. I'm not going anywhere."

His words filled me with a sense of warmth and reassurance. I knew he was right. I couldn't neglect my duties, but I also deserved to be happy.

"I love you," I said, knowing that those three words held so much weight.

"I love you too," he replied, pressing a soft kiss to my forehead.

We stood there for a few more moments, holding each other and enjoying the peace, before we both knew we had to leave.

"I'll see you after the ceremony," I said, giving him one last kiss before pulling away.

"Good luck," he said, his eyes filled with love and pride.

I smiled at him before reluctantly making my way back to my quarters to get ready for the coronation ceremony.

As I slipped back into my chambers, Avery stood there with her arms crossed against her chest and a knowing look in her eyes. "Sneaking out to see a certain someone?" she teased.

"Maybe." I laughed while she helped me get ready.

Afterwards, Avery and I stood side-by-side, staring at ourselves in one of the floor length mirrors that hung in my room.

I glanced over at Avery, her hair cascading down her back from the elaborate half-up do that had taken far too long to create. While mine was woven into a braided crown atop my head. We were both wearing floor-length gowns, hers a shimmering silver and mine a glimmering gold.

"You ready?" I asked.

"As ready as I can be," she replied.

I linked my arm through hers, and we made our way to the grand hall where the ceremony was to take place.

As we entered the hall, the room fell silent. We could feel the weight of every eye in the room upon us, and I couldn't help but feel a sense of pride and responsibility settle over me. I wasn't sure if this day would ever come; I definitely never imagined it would happen like this.

The hall was filled to the brim with dignitaries from all over Caelestia, as well as our closest friends and family.

We made our way down the aisle, every eye in the room on us. I did not need to have Avery's telepathy to know that they were all wondering if we could fulfill the expectations of leading Soluna as its new rulers. I tried to block out the thoughts and instead focused on Wesley's reassuring gaze from where he stood at the front of the hall.

As we reached the dais where our thrones were set, the council members stood up and announced our ascension to the throne. We both took a deep breath and rose onto our thrones, feeling a rush of emotions from this monumental moment.

The ceremony began with speeches from important figures in Caelestia and then quickly moved to our coronation oaths that we would both swear before taking our places as queens.

Finally, it was time for us to be officially crowned the Queens of Soluna by placing the golden crowns atop our heads simultaneously. I knew that the next few years would be filled with challenges and difficult decisions, but I was ready to face them head-on. I was determined to be the best queen I could be, for myself, for the people of Soluna, and for Wesley.

"Long live Queen Avery and Queen Amara!" they proclaimed, their voices echoing throughout the hall.

We looked out at the sea of faces, feeling the weight of their expectations upon us but also their love and support. It was a moment we would never forget.

As the ceremony came to a close, Avery and I made our way down from the dais to greet our guests. We shook hands, exchanged pleasantries, and accepted congratulations from all who approached us. But my eyes never left Wesley's, who stood in the back of the room, watching me with a mixture of pride and adoration.

I couldn't wait to finally be alone with him, to celebrate this momentous occasion with him by my side. But as the night wore on, it became clear that wouldn't be possible. There were too many guests, too many obligations, and too many things that needed our attention.

By the time the last of the guests had left, I was exhausted both physically and emotionally. But as I made my way to my chambers, I saw that Wesley was still waiting for me just outside the hall, a soft smile on his face.

"Hey there," he said as I approached him.

"Hey yourself," I replied, trying not to let my exhaustion show.

He took my hand and led me to a room that was not my own, but just down the hall from it. He pushed the door open, and we stepped inside. It was warm and inviting, with a blazing fire in the hearth and a plush bed in the centre of the room.

"Whose room is this?" I asked.

He shrugged. "I talked to Lawrence, and we agreed it might be easier on you if I had a room a little closer to yours."

I turned back to him, and he spoke again.

"I thought we could have a little celebration of our own," he said, his voice low.

My heart skipped a beat as I realized what he meant. He wrapped his arms around me, holding me tight against him. I could feel his heartbeat through his chest as he whispered in my ear.

"You were amazing," he said softly. "I'm so proud of you."

I looked up at him, a smile spreading across my face. "I couldn't have done it without you," I replied, reaching up to kiss him. As our lips met, I felt a rush of desire wash over me. It had been so long since we had been intimate, and I was desperate for his touch.

Wesley seemed to sense my need; he lifted me up and carried me to the bed.

CHAPTER TWENTY-SIX

Avery

As the reception began to die down, I sat with my mom at one of the tables, sipping champagne as the few guests that remained danced around, enjoying the festivities. It was a relief to finally let loose and celebrate with the people we loved. I was so glad when I found out she was able to make it. 'Wouldn't miss it for the world, whichever world it was.' she'd said when I invited her.

"Congratulations, my Queen," a deep voice said from behind us.

I turned to find Xander standing there, a proud smile on his face.

"Thank you." I smiled back.

"I'm proud of you," he said, taking a seat next to me.

239

My mom and I both smiled at him, grateful for his unwavering support.

"Are you enjoying the party?" my mom asked while taking another sip of her drink.

"I am," he replied. "But I'd rather dance with my queen, if you don't mind me stealing her away for a while."

My heart skipped a beat at his words, and I stood up, taking his hand. As other couples swayed to the music, we made our way to the dance floor. As Xander pulled me closer, I could feel the heat of his body against mine. His hand was strong against my lower back, guiding me in the dance. We moved together as if we were one, lost in the magic of the moment.

"You were amazing up there," he said, his voice low and intimate.

"Thank you," I replied, resting my head against his chest. "But I couldn't have done it without Amara."

"She's lucky to have you." His voice was filled with admiration.

We danced for a while, lost in our own little world. But as the song came to an end, Xander pulled away from me, his eyes searching mine.

"Can I show you something?" he asked, his voice low.

I nodded, intrigued. Xander led me out of the grand hall and into a small courtyard, where the stars were shining down on us like diamonds in the sky.

"This is beautiful," I breathed, taking in the sight before me.

"I thought you might like it," Xander said, smiling at me.

We walked through the courtyard hand in hand, enjoying the peaceful atmosphere. But as we rounded a corner, we came to the small pond that had been tucked away. The water was still and calm, reflecting the stars above.

Suddenly, Xander stopped and turned to face me, his eyes intense.

"Avery, I need to tell you something," he said.

I felt a sudden pang of anxiety in my chest, unsure of what he was about to say.

"What is it?" I asked, my voice barely above a whisper.

"I need to go back to Coldoria, and I don't know how long I will be gone for this time."

My heart sank at his words, but I knew that duty called for him just as it did for me and Amara. I stepped closer to him, placing a hand on his chest.

"I understand," I said, trying to keep my voice steady. "I'll miss you, but I'll always be here waiting for you."

Xander took my hand and brought it to his lips, kissing it softly.

"I'll miss you too," he said. "But I promise to come back to you as soon as possible."

I nodded, tears welling up in my eyes. "How soon do you have to leave?"

"Tomorrow morning," he replied, his voice heavy with regret.

I took a deep breath, trying to steel myself for the inevitable goodbye. But Xander wasn't finished yet.

"However," he said, a mischievous glint in his eye. "I was thinking we could make the most of tonight."

Before I could even respond, he pulled me into a deep kiss, his hands roaming over my body. I moaned softly against his lips, my own desire rising to meet his.

We made our way back to the grand hall, unable to keep our hands off each other. Xander led me to a secluded corner of the room, hidden by velvet drapes. As he pushed me against the wall, I felt a thrill of excitement course through me.

We kissed hungrily, our bodies pressed tightly together.

"I love you, Avery," he whispered against my lips.

"I love you too, Xander."

He pulled away from me then, his eyes burning into mine. "How can I make tonight last forever?" he asked, his voice raw with emotion.

I couldn't answer him, too overcome by my own desire for him. He lifted me up, carrying me down the hall to his room. As he pushed the door open, I felt my heart race at the thought of what was about to happen.

I woke up the next morning as the last rays of sunlight were peeking out through the window. I groaned, rolling over, but suddenly realized Xander wasn't in bed next to me. I sat up slowly, rubbing my eyes. I was still exhausted from the night before, though the memories of what we had done would be burned in my memory forever. My heart racing at the thought of him having left without waking me up.

"You're up," I heard him say as he strode into the room.

I smiled at him, relief flooding through me at the sound of his voice. "I was worried you'd left without saying goodbye."

"I wouldn't do that to you," he replied, his voice gentle. He sat down on the bed next to me, cupping my face in his hands.

He leaned forward, kissing me deeply. I smiled against his lips, pressing my body closer to his briefly before pulling away.

"Good, because I have something for you."

Xander's eyes widened in surprise. "You do?" he asked.

I nodded, reaching up to unclasp the silver crescent moon necklace I always wore. "I wanted to give you something to remember me by."

Xander traced his fingers down my arm as I placed the necklace against his chest. "I'm sure I'll miss you just as much as you'll miss this while I'm away," he said, holding onto the pendant.

I smiled, kissing him once more. "I love you," I said, as tears filled my eyes.

"I love you too, Avery," he replied, his voice soft.

Xander wrapped his arm around my waist, pulling me in close. He kissed me again, and I felt my heartbeat quicken against him. I laughed as we pulled away from each other temporarily to catch our breath.

"I only wish we could spend another day in bed," I said, a sly grin on my face.

Xander laughed, leaning forward to kiss the tip of my nose. "I'm tempted to call off the trip," he replied, a mischievous look on his face.

I rolled my eyes, though inside I would have been more than happy to do just that. "Unfortunately, your people need you," I said, smiling sadly at him.

"I know," he replied, his face full of regret.

We sat there for a little while, enjoying the feeling of being together. But finally, Xander had to go. I walked him to the castle gates, where a carriage was waiting for him. Xander took my hands in his, holding them tightly against him.

"I'll see you soon," he said softly.

"I'll be waiting," I replied, my eyes filling with tears.

He leaned in close, kissing me one last time. "I love you."

"I love you too," I whispered against his lips, not wanting to let him go.

When we pulled away from each other, Xander gave me one last, longing look before walking away.

I stood there for a moment, watching him walk away, before turning around and walking back into the castle. I made my way to my room, wishing I could run after him and stop him from leaving. But I knew he needed to be there. He had left his kingdom in such a rush to save mine and the people trapped within the Shadow Lands. He had gone against his father and challenged him for the throne. He needed to deal with the fallout and his people, and I knew that was more important than anything.

Sitting down at my mirror, I ran a brush through my hair. I stared at my reflection for a while, trying to ignore the emptiness I saw in my own eyes. I thought about the night before, laughing to myself as I thought of the look on Xander's face when I had given him my necklace this morning. I thought of how he had held onto me, like he was afraid I would slip away if he let go. I thought about how he told me he loved me one last time before walking away. Finally, I started crying.

I wiped the tears from my eyes, hoping that I had gotten them out of my system. But the more I thought about Xander, the more I cried. I wasn't sure if it was from sadness or happiness, but I just couldn't stop. I glanced at the mirror, knowing that I looked horrible and that I had to pull myself together. I decided to go for a walk around the grounds to clear my head. I stepped out into the hallway, trying to ignore how everything looked so different without Xander there.

Rounding a corner, I smacked right into someone, nearly knocking them and myself to the ground.

"I am so sorry," I mumbled.

"You really need to start paying attention when you take corners," Hazel laughed.

"You didn't go with him?" I blinked in surprise.

"No," she said, her dark curls bouncing as she shook her head. "I figured I'd stay here until everything was sorted out with our father."

"I'm so glad," I said, pulling her into a tight hug.

"I'm glad I stayed too," she said, her eyes shining.

I smiled, hoping she wouldn't notice my red, puffy eyes. "You look like you've been crying," she said, her eyes widening in concern.

"I'm just really emotional lately," I lied, trying to cover up how I really felt.

She nodded, though I could tell she didn't believe me. "You can tell me, you know," she said, her soft smile sincere.

"I just miss him," I whispered.

We made our way out to the garden, standing at the top of the steps leading down to the garden. Hazel sat down on one of the benches, patting the spot next to her in invitation.

"I had no idea how hard it would be," I said quietly as I sat down next to her. "I knew he would have to leave, but I didn't think it would hurt so much."

"I can imagine," she said, her lips turned down.

"I just wish he didn't have to go so soon," I said, staring down at my hands that were clasped together in my lap.

Hazel reached over, squeezing my hand. "I know," she said, her voice full of understanding. "Is there anything I can do?"

"I don't know," I said, shaking my head. "You're such a great friend, you know that?"

"Oh, I've been told a time or two," she winked, and I snorted out a laugh in response.

"So…" I dragged out. "Any new developments in your love life?" I teased, bumping my shoulder against hers.

"Maybe," she laughed again.

I gasped dramatically. "Don't tell me that's the real reason you wanted to stay here in Soluna. And here I thought it was because of me."

"Please, you're with my brother. Gross." She made a fake gagging sound, and we both burst out into laughter.

"You know I love you," I said, nudging her.

"Yeah, yeah," she laughed, nudging me back. When we finally settled down, she sighed. "I just don't want to say anything before I'm ready, you know."

"I understand," I replied. "Is it serious?"

She shrugged. "Maybe."

"Is it someone I know?" I asked, already guessing.

"Could be," she said, her eyes twinkling. I opened my mouth to guess, but she put her hand up, stopping me. "No, don't even go there."

I stuck my tongue out at her, and she started laughing again.

"Well, I don't care who it is, as long as you're happy."

"I am," she smiled as she looked out into the garden.

As we sat there in silence, enjoying the peace and serenity of the garden, I couldn't stop thinking about Xander. I wanted to be with him so badly that it hurt. I longed to feel his touch, his embrace, his lips on mine. But I knew that I had to be patient. Xander had duties to attend to, and I had to respect that.

Suddenly, Hazel nudged me with her elbow, pulling me out of my thoughts. "Look," she said, pointing to the far corner of the garden.

I followed her gaze and saw a couple sitting on a bench, lost in each other's arms. The woman's familiar long, blonde hair cascaded down her back. They looked so happy, so in love.

"You know," I said, pulling Hazel's attention away from the couple. "We could probably use a new Duchess of Caelia, if you want to stay here permanently."

"You don't say." She grinned.

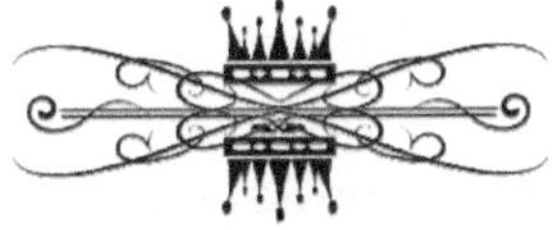

The sun cast a warm glow over Soluna, its rays dancing on the newly polished surfaces of the castle. The war was over, and a sense of peace had settled over the kingdom. Amara and I stood on the balcony of the room we had shared, looking out at the kingdom we now co-ruled as queens.

"It's a beautiful day," Amara said, her eyes reflecting the calm after the storm. "Hard to believe that last week we were in the midst of battle."

I nodded, the weight of the crown on my head a constant reminder of the responsibilities that now rested upon us. "We did it, Amara. We brought peace to Soluna and the Shadow Lands." Which used to be part of Soluna and was now once again a part of our kingdom.

She smiled, a mix of pride and relief in her expression. "Co-queens. Who would've thought?"

"Not me, that's for sure," I replied, chuckling. The journey from an ordinary life in the mortal world to being crowned as a queen was nothing short of extraordinary.

Amara's gaze turned to the bustling courtyard below, where the people of Soluna went about their daily lives. "Our people are resilient. Despite the darkness that tried to consume us, they stood strong. And now, they can rebuild."

"It's a new beginning for Soluna," I said, my heart swelling with a sense of hope. "And for us."

Amara turned to me, her eyes searching mine. "Avery, I know this is a lot to take in. From discovering your true identity to leading a kingdom. But I have faith in you. In both of us."

I smiled, grateful for her unwavering support. "I couldn't have asked for a better sister. And co-queen."

She bumped her shoulder against mine playfully. "Get used to it, Your Highness. We have a kingdom to run."

As we returned inside and descended the grand staircase, the castle staff greeted us with smiles and cheers. The air was filled with a sense of celebration, a reflection of the joy that had replaced the recent darkness.

In the throne room, our thrones stood side by side, symbols of our shared rule. Mine with a moon in different phases etched along the top, and Amara's with a swirling sun. Amara and I took our seats, acknowledging the gathered courtiers and advisors. The weight of the crown felt significant, but with Amara by my side, I knew we could face anything.

As the day unfolded, we delved into the intricacies of governance, making decisions that would shape the future of Soluna. The responsibilities were immense, but the bond between Amara and me served as a guiding force. I was thankful for Lawrence, as he had offered to help teach me everything.

Later that evening, as the sun dipped below the horizon, Amara and I found ourselves on the balcony once again. The sky was painted in hues of orange and pink, a serene backdrop to our newfound roles.

"We did it," Amara said, breaking the comfortable silence. "We're queens."

I chuckled. "Queens who need to figure out how to rule a kingdom."

"We'll learn together," Amara reassured, her gaze fixed on the horizon. "And we have each other. That's what matters."

I nodded, knowing that the journey ahead would be challenging but also filled with moments of sisterly support and shared victories. As the stars began to twinkle in the evening sky, I couldn't help but feel grateful for the extraordinary path that had led me to this moment, standing beside my sister, co-queen of Soluna.

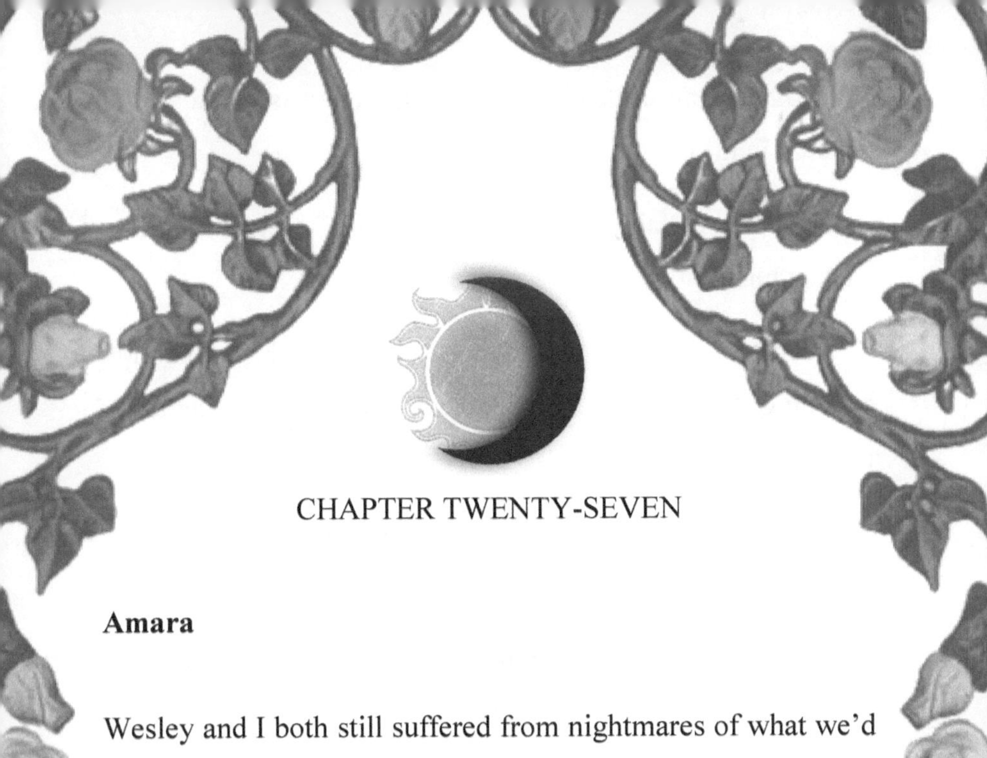

CHAPTER TWENTY-SEVEN

Amara

Wesley and I both still suffered from nightmares of what we'd been through. But we were getting through it together. We'd both been through so much, and it was a comfort to know that we had each other to lean on. We had come a long way since we'd first met so many years ago. We were just kids back then, dreaming of what life could have been like now. Back then, I swore I'd never be queen.

But now, as I stared out from my bedroom balcony overlooking the kingdom, I realized that being queen wasn't so bad after all. It came with its challenges, of course, but it also came with the ability to make a difference in people's lives. And that was something that I had always wanted to do.

"Thinking about taking over the world again?" Wesley's voice pulled me out of my thoughts, and I turned to look at him.

He had a teasing smile on his face, but there was also a hint of concern in his eyes.

"Just thinking about how far we've come," I replied, smiling back at him.

"Yeah, we have come a long way," he said, his expression softening. "I'm proud of you, Amara. You've done an amazing job."

My cheeks heated up at his praise. "Thanks," I said softly.

He stepped closer to me, wrapping his arms around my waist. "I love you," he whispered into my ear, and I felt my heart skip a beat.

"I love you too," I said, turning around to face him. We shared a soft, tender kiss.

"I never thought I could be this happy," he said, his eyes locked on mine.

I smiled. "Me neither."

We stood there for a while, just enjoying each other's company. Eventually, we both knew it was time to get back to work. There were still so many issues to address, problems to solve, and people to help.

As we made our way back inside, I found myself thinking about the future and what it held for us. I knew there would be more challenges, more struggles, but I also knew that as long as we had each other, we could get through anything.

"I have a surprise for you tonight," he said against my lips as he kissed me once more.

"A surprise?" I lifted a brow, waiting for him to elaborate.

He nodded. "Meet me in the stables later," he laughed as he ran out the door.

I shook my head as I followed after him. He was nowhere in sight as I stepped into the corridor, so I went on about my day.

As the day went by, I couldn't help but feel excited about the surprise Wesley had planned for me. I went about my day, dealing with various tasks and attending to the needs of the kingdom, but my mind kept wandering back to what he had said earlier.

As night fell, I made my way to the stables, wondering what I would find there. When I arrived, the stables were empty.

"Wes," I called out as I searched for him.

"Surprise!" He yelled out.

My gaze shot upwards, and I saw him clinging to the wooden beams. His eyes sparkled in the dim light as he let go, hurtling through the air with arms outstretched. In the seconds before he crashed into me, I could do nothing but scream. We tumbled across the floor, finally coming to a standstill with him hovering above me, grinning triumphantly.

"You have to always be prepared," he teased before kissing me.

My lips met his in a passionate kiss, and as I felt his body relax. With one hand, I pushed him firmly to his back, and in a swift motion, I was now straddling him on the ground.

He cupped my cheeks in his calloused hands, barely giving me time to breathe before pressing his lips against mine again. I felt all of my resistance melt away as his kiss turned deeper.

"Marry me," he murmured against my lips.

My heart skipped a beat at his words. I pulled back, staring at him in shock. "What?" I whispered, almost afraid to believe what I had just heard.

"Marry me," he repeated, taking my hand in his. "I want to spend the rest of my life with you, Amara. I want to grow old with you. I want to wake up every morning and see your face. I want to hold you close every night. I want to be yours forever."

Tears prickled at the corners of my eyes as I looked down at him. I had never been so sure of anything in my life. "Yes," I whispered, my heart overflowing with love and happiness.

"Yes?" he asked, his eyes shining with joy.

"Yes," I repeated, throwing my arms around him. "I will marry you, Wesley."

He hugged me back tightly, and we stayed like that for a while, just revelling in the moment. It was like I was seeing everything in a new light; the world was brighter and more beautiful than ever before. All of our struggles, all of our hardships, had led us to this moment. I knew it wouldn't be easy, being queen and being married, but it was worth it. For Wesley, it was worth it.

As we broke apart, Wesley pulled something out of his pocket. It was a small box. He opened it to reveal a beautiful diamond ring. It sparkled in the dim light of the stables.

"It was my mom's," he whispered.

"It's beautiful."

"Just like you," he said, smiling.

I slipped the ring onto my finger, and it fit perfectly. It was like it was meant to be there all along.

"I can't wait to spend the rest of my life with you," I said, leaning in to kiss him again.

"Me too," he said, kissing me back. "Now, let's go celebrate."

We stood up and made our way out of the stables, hand in hand. The night air was crisp and cool, and stars sparkled in the sky overhead.

As we walked, I couldn't help but feel grateful for everything I had. For Wesley, for our love, for the kingdom that I was able to help, and for the future that lay ahead of us.

We made our way to the royal gardens, where we found a small table set up with candles and a bottle of wine. Wesley had thought of everything, and it made my heart swell with love for him even more.

We sat down, and he poured us each a glass of wine. We talked, laughed, and reminisced about all the good times we had shared. It was like nothing could touch us, like the world was ours for the taking.

As we finished our meal, Wesley stood up and offered me his hand.

"May I have this dance?" he asked.

I smiled and took his hand, letting him lead me to the centre of the garden. Soft music played in the background, and I felt like I was in a dream.

He pulled me close, and we began to move together in perfect harmony. I closed my eyes, savouring the feeling of being in his arms.

"I love you," he whispered as we swayed back and forth.

"I love you too," I responded, resting my head on his shoulder.

We danced for what felt like hours, lost in our own world.

Wesley eventually walked me back to my quarters, where I called it a night. As much as I wanted to spend the night with him in his rooms, I wanted to see Avery and tell her about what just happened. And I wanted to make sure she was okay.

When I opened the doors to my room, I found Avery sitting at the table, staring out the window. She looked up as I entered, and I could see the sadness in her eyes.

"Hey," I said softly, walking over to her.

"Hey," she mumbled.

"What's wrong?" I asked, sitting down next to her.

"It's just..." she trailed off, biting her lip. "I miss him."

"I know," I said, wrapping my arm around her shoulders. "But Xander will be back soon enough."

"I hope so," she whispered, resting her head on my shoulder. "I just hate being away from him."

"I understand," I said, stroking her hair. "But you know he loves you, right? And he'll be back as soon as he can."

"I know," she said, sighing. "It's just hard, you know?"

"I do," I replied, leaning my head against hers. "But we'll get through this. Together."

"I know." She smiled weakly. "Thank you, Amara."

"Always," I said, squeezing her shoulder. I opened my mouth to tell her about Wesley but hesitated for a moment. I didn't want to make her feel worse.

"What is it?" she asked.

I shook my head. "It's nothing."

"It's not nothing. You can tell me anything," she insisted.

"Wesley asked me to marry him." I sighed.

Her eyes widened. "And you said no?"

"What? No, I said yes."

"But you wanted to say no?" She asked again, her brows furrowing slightly.

"No, I wanted to say yes."

"So why are you sad?"

"Because you're sad!" I said, a little too loudly, and quickly slapped my hand over my mouth at the outburst.

She laughed. "You don't have to hide your happiness just because I'm sad. I *want* you to be happy! *I* am happy for you," she said, pulling me into a tight embrace.

"I am happy," I murmured into her hair as I hugged her back.

CHAPTER TWENTY-EIGHT

Avery

As the days passed, we had so much to do that it was hard to find a moment to breathe. The preparations for the wedding were in full swing, and every detail needed to be perfect. Amara was busy with meetings and dress fittings, while I helped as much as I could with the decorations and guest arrangements. Not only that, but I was co-ruler of an entire kingdom now. Lawrence was giving me lessons in everything. I was so grateful to have him and Amara's help in all of this.

In the back of my mind, though, I couldn't shake the feeling of missing Xander. It had been weeks since he had left, and I was starting to feel the weight of his absence. I missed his touch, his smell, his voice. I missed everything about him.

Amara was determined to make it the perfect day, and Wesley was more than happy to go along with her every whim.

As we worked, I couldn't help but feel a pang of jealousy. I wanted what they had—a love so strong that it was palpable. Xander and I had been together for such a short time; it wasn't like that. We didn't have the luxury of time to truly get to know each other. We were forced to jump into a relationship when we were barely acquaintances.

But despite my envy, I was genuinely happy for my sister. She deserved all the happiness in the world, and Wesley seemed to be the one to give it to her.

One day, as we were taking a break from our busy schedules, Lawrence approached us with a serious look on his face.

"Ladies, I need to discuss something with you," he said, gesturing for us to follow him to his study.

We exchanged worried glances before obediently following him to his study. Once inside, Lawrence closed the door behind us and turned to face us.

"I have received word from Coldoria," Lawrence continued, and my heart skipped a beat as I eyed the now unsealed letter in his hand. "King Alexander has stepped down, and Xander has been crowned king."

"That's great," I practically cheered, jumping out of my seat, but the sad expression Lawrence wore on his face told me there was more to it. I sat back down in my chair and cleared my throat. "Sorry, please continue."

He nodded. "He has called off the official wedding and merging of our kingdoms but wishes to remain allies."

"Oh." I breathed.

"What an asshole," Amara murmured from the seat next to me.

"Was there anything else in the letter?" I asked hopefully, but Lawrence just shook his head slightly as he placed the letter down on his desk.

"That was the main point of the letter, but I'm sure there will be more information soon," Lawrence said with a sigh. "I'm sorry, Avery. I know how much this must hurt for you."

I didn't really know where this left Xander and I. We never got to discuss this; I wished he would have talked to me first. I mean, I wasn't exactly sure if I was ready to get married either, but I think I deserved more than some letter that wasn't even addressed to me.

Tears prickled at the corners of my eyes, but I refused to let them fall. I had to be strong, both for myself and for my people.

"It's okay," I said, forcing a smile. "At least we'll still have an alliance."

"Right," Amara agreed, but I could tell that she was just as sad as I was, and probably angrier.

"We'll figure it out," Lawrence said, putting a reassuring hand on my shoulder. "But for now, we need to focus on Amara's wedding."

I nodded, trying to push the news to the back of my mind. There would be time to deal with it later, but for now, we had a wedding to plan.

We left Lawrence's study, and I made my way back to my room, needing some time alone to process everything. As soon as I closed the door behind me, I crumbled onto the bed and let the tears flow freely.

I was so lost in my thoughts that I flinched as someone knocked on my door.

Wiping the tears from my eyes, I pulled myself out of bed, wondering who it was. *Could it be too much to ask for it to be Xander?* I thought as I dragged my feet towards the door.

Hazel stood on the other side of the door, a sad smile on her face. "Avery, may I come in?" she asked softly.

I nodded, opening the door wider for her. She stepped inside and closed the door behind her.

Hazel had been a constant source of comfort and support over the past few weeks, and I was grateful to have her as a friend.

She sat down next to me on the bed, taking my hand in hers. "I heard about Xander," she said gently.

I just nodded again, unable to speak.

"Gods, he's such a jerk sometimes. I know everything must have happened so quickly for him. *I* didn't even get to attend his coronation, and I'm his sister. I… I'm just so sorry, Avery," she said, squeezing my hand.

"I just wish he would have talked to me about it first," I said, feeling a mix of anger and sadness.

"I understand," she said, giving my back a gentle rub. "It's okay to not be okay. But remember, you have people who love you and will support you no matter what. Maybe this is for the best. You both have a lot on your plates right now, and maybe it's better to focus on your individual kingdoms for now."

"Maybe." I sighed, leaning my head against her shoulder.

We sat there in silence for a few moments before Hazel pulled away slightly, looking at me with a serious expression.

"There's something else I need to tell you," she said, "something I've been meaning to tell you for weeks now."

"What is it?" I asked, worried by the seriousness of her tone.

"I was going to wait until after the wedding, but a letter arrived from Xander's army headquarters this morning." She paused, looking as though she was struggling to find the words to continue. "I just want you to be prepared."

"Prepared for what?" I asked, my heartbeat accelerating as panic started to set in.

"There's been some trouble going on in Coldoria. I don't know all the details, but from what I receive, it's nothing to worry about; Xander has it all under control now," she explained.

"What kind of situation?" I asked, feeling a tinge of concern rush through me.

"Just some of the council and royal guard that were still loyal to my father," she said with a sigh. "They don't agree with Xander's decision to step down and are causing some trouble. But like I said, Xander is taking care of it."

I nodded, not sure what to say. It seemed like the troubles just kept coming, one after the other. I wondered if this was my fate—to never have a moment of peace.

"Thank you for telling me," I finally said, grateful for her honesty.

"Of course," she said, giving my hand a final squeeze before getting up from the bed. "Now, we should get back to the wedding planning. We can't let this news ruin Amara's big day."

I nodded again, wiping away the last of my tears. Hazel was right; we couldn't let this news ruin everything. We had a wedding to plan and a kingdom to run.

I smiled, feeling a sense of gratitude wash over me as I stood up from the bed and followed Hazel out of my room. Even though things with Xander were uncertain, I knew that I had friends and family who would always have my back.

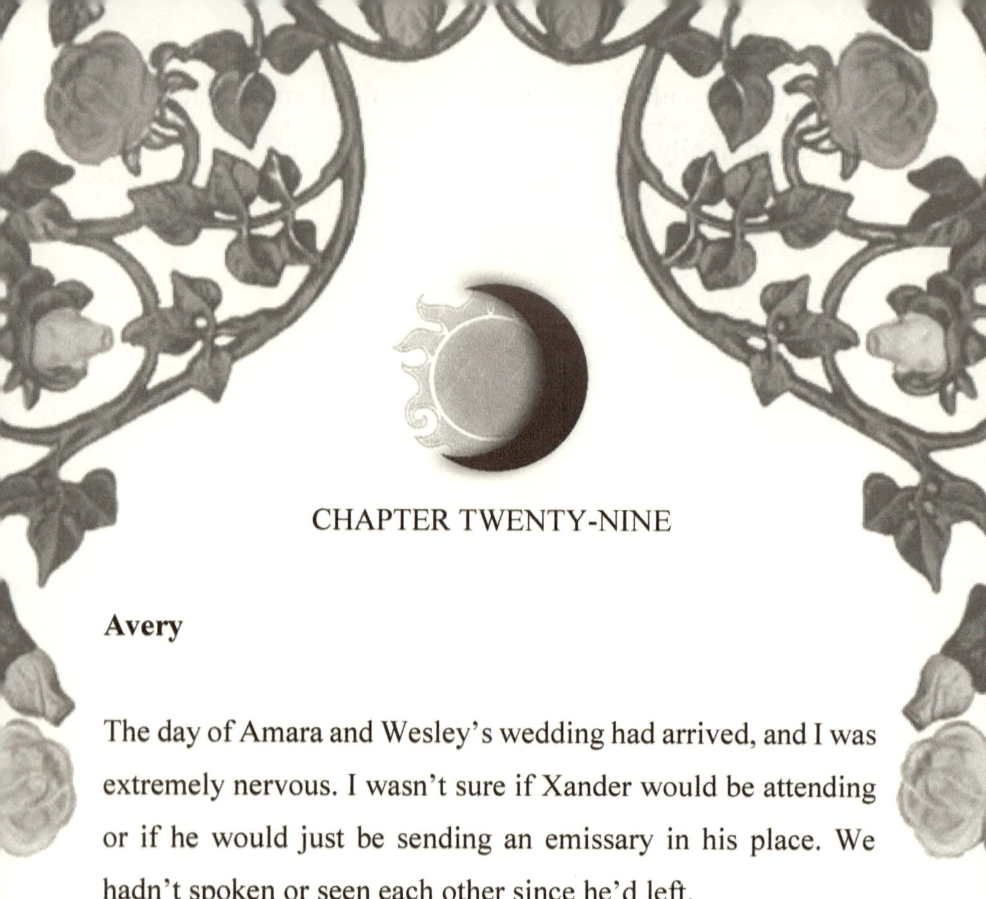

CHAPTER TWENTY-NINE

Avery

The day of Amara and Wesley's wedding had arrived, and I was extremely nervous. I wasn't sure if Xander would be attending or if he would just be sending an emissary in his place. We hadn't spoken or seen each other since he'd left.

As I walked through the halls of the palace towards the grand ballroom, I couldn't help but feel a sense of emptiness in my chest. It was strange not having Xander by my side.

When I entered the ballroom, I slowly made my way down the aisle, lost in my own thoughts. What was Xander doing right now? Was he thinking of me? My thoughts were quickly interrupted as I noticed a familiar figure seated in the front row. It was Xander, dressed in his royal regalia. My heart skipped a beat as I walked past him and took my place at the front, waiting for Amara to enter.

I could feel the tension in the air between us. We obviously couldn't say anything to each other during the ceremony, and I refused to look his way, but I felt his gaze burning into me.

Amara finally entered the room, looking absolutely stunning in her long, laced wedding gown. She looked like a true queen, and I couldn't help but feel a sense of pride for my twin sister.

As the ceremony continued, I caved and stole some glances at Xander every now and then. He looked as handsome as ever, his dark hair styled perfectly, and his sharp jawline accentuated by the light filtering off the sun through the large windows.

I tried my best to focus on Amara and Wesley's vows, but my mind kept drifting back to Xander. I wondered what he was thinking, if he regretted his decision to go. If he missed me as desperately as I missed him. Why he hadn't written to me.

When the ceremony ended, I watched as Amara and Wesley shared their first kiss as husband and wife. It was a beautiful moment, and a tear slid down my cheek at the pure joy that radiated from the two of them.

As Wesley lifted Amara into his arms and carried her down the aisle, the guests let out another round of cheers, and I clapped along with them.

The guests began to mingle and celebrate, and I found myself avoiding Xander, unsure of what to say to him. But as I made my way towards the refreshment table, he appeared by my side.

"Avery," he said softly, his eyes searching mine.

"Xander," I said, trying to keep my voice steady.

"You've grown more beautiful since the last time I saw you," he said, his eyes narrowing slightly.

"How are you?" I asked, deciding to ignore his last comment.

"Fine," he replied. I looked up at him and was surprised to see a hint of annoyance in his eyes.

"What's wrong?" I asked.

"I just… I thought you would have at least written back to me by now," he said. "I thought you'd at least want to know how things were going, how I was handling everything."

"Written back? What was I supposed to say? Sorry you called off the wedding. Glad you still want to be allies. How's things in Coldoria going? Hope you're happy now," I snapped, feeling a burst of anger inside me. "What did you expect, Xander? You wrote without any explanation, without even talking to me first."

"I *did* write to you first, and I wasn't engaged to you; I was engaged to Amara. I had to cancel the arrangement so we could be here today." He gestured around us, like I forgot where we were.

"I know where we are!" I fired back.

He scoffed. "I figured you'd be happy."

"Happy? Why would I be happy? You wrote a letter that Lawrence had to read to me. I wasn't even sure where that left us. Was it over then? Are we over now? You didn't tell me anything!"

"What are you talking about? Didn't you get my other letters?" His brows furrowed slightly.

"What other letters?"

"The ones I sent after I left. The ones where I explained everything," he paused, his eyes searching mine for any hint of recognition.

"I didn't receive any other letters," I said, feeling a sense of confusion wash over me. "I thought you just left without a word."

"I sent you letters every week, but I never received any response," he said, looking hurt.

"I don't understand. I never got any other letters," I said, feeling a sense of regret for not knowing the truth sooner.

"I don't know what happened to them," he said, his voice softening. "But I do know that I miss you, Avery. I miss being with you, and I want to try again."

I looked up at him, feeling a sense of hope flutter in my chest. "Try what?"

"Us. Our relationship," he said, his eyes searching mine. "I know things have been difficult, but I want to make it work. I meant what I said before I left. Avery, I love you," he said, his voice barely above a whisper.

I felt my heart skip a beat, the world around us fading away as I looked into his eyes. "I love you too, Xander," I said, tears forming in my eyes.

He pulled me into a tight embrace, holding me close as we both cried happy tears. The guests around us continued to celebrate, but in that moment, it was just the two of us, lost in our love for each other.

As we pulled away from each other, Xander took my hand in his. "Let's start over," he said, a smile spreading across his face.

I smiled back at him, feeling a weight lift off my shoulders. "Okay," I said, nodding my head.

We spent the rest of the wedding celebration together, dancing and talking about our future. We had a lot of work to do and things to figure out, but we were willing to do whatever it took.

As the night came to a close, Xander took my hand and led me outside into the palace gardens. The moon was high in the sky, casting a soft glow over the flowers and trees around us. Xander pulled me close to him, wrapping his arms around my waist.

"I've missed you," he said, his voice soft and tender.

"I've missed you too," I replied, looking up at him.

He leaned in, pressing his lips against mine in a gentle kiss. I wrapped my arms around his neck, deepening the kiss as the passion between us ignited. We broke apart, gasping for air, and Xander looked at me with a fire in his eyes.

"Come with me back to Coldoria or ask me to stay here. I don't care. I just want to be with you," he said, his voice filled with desire.

I stared into his eyes, feeling the intensity of his love. I knew what I wanted.

"I'll come with you," I said, a smile spreading across my face.

Xander's face lit up with joy, and he pulled me into another kiss.

I gave into his kiss for a moment before pulling away again. "But not forever; I have a kingdom to run too. But I want to make it work," I said, looking at him with determination.

"Of course, we'll figure it out," he said, a grin spreading across his face.

We spent the rest of the night in each other's arms, lost in the passion of our love and planning our future together. The moonlight sparkled through the trees, adding a special glow to the moment. We knew it wouldn't be easy, but we were willing to face whatever challenges came our way. And I knew that our love was just beginning.

EPILOGUE

Avery

It had been five years since that night in the palace gardens. Xander and I had been through a lot together since then, but our love has only grown stronger. We split our time between Coldoria and Soluna. And there may have been a few visits to the mortal world as well.

Once Xander and I had our first daughter, my mom insisted on moving here, not that I objected. We'd faced challenges, of course. Disagreements about how to rule our kingdoms, long periods of time apart, and even a few attempts on our lives. But we'd faced them all together, and our love had never faltered.

As I watched our daughter, Callie, play in the gardens of the Soluna palace, I couldn't help but feel grateful for everything we'd been through. Xander came up behind me, wrapping his arms around my waist as we both watched our daughter with pride.

"I can't believe she's already three," he said, his voice filled with wonder.

"I know," I said, smiling up at him. "It feels like just yesterday we were planning our wedding."

"And now we're ruling two kingdoms and raising a family together," he said, a smile spreading across his face.

"Life has a funny way of working out," I said, leaning into his embrace.

"I'm just grateful that I get to share it all with you," he said, pressing a kiss to my temple.

"Me too," I said, feeling my heart swell with love.

We spent the rest of the afternoon playing with our daughter in the gardens, enjoying the simple pleasures of life. Amara and Wesley came running up to join us.

"Here comes your favourite uncle," Wesley said as he picked Callie up and swung her around in his arms.

"You're her only uncle," Amara said bitterly as Callie refused to pick a favourite between her, Hazel, and Larina.

"Still the favourite though," he shouted back before finally putting Callie back down.

Amara and Wesley never had any kids of their own; they'd said they were more than happy to be the fun aunts and uncles and let Callie be the next heir to both Soluna and Coldoria.

As I watched our family play together, I knew that we were exactly where we were meant to be. We had faced so many challenges, but we had come out stronger on the other side.

"Hey, come on," Xander said, taking my hand. "Let's go for a walk."

I nodded, following him as we walked through the gardens, hand in hand. The sun was setting, casting a warm glow over everything around us. As we walked, Xander stopped, turning to face me.

"I've been thinking," he said, his eyes meeting mine. "I want to do something special for our anniversary this year. Something big."

I raised an eyebrow, curious and excited. "Really? What did you have in mind?"

Xander grinned, his eyes sparkling. "I was thinking about taking a trip. Just the two of us. Maybe to the mortal realm. I heard there's a beautiful beach there that I'd love to take you to," he said, his voice filled with excitement.

I smiled, feeling my heart flutter with excitement. "I'd love that," I said, leaning in to kiss him.

As our lips met, I felt the same rush of passion that I had felt when we first kissed. Our love had only grown stronger over the years, and I knew that it would continue to do so.

I pulled away, my eyes meeting his.

"I love you," I said, my voice filled with emotion.

"I love you too," he replied, his own voice filled with the same intensity.

We stood there for a moment, lost in our love for each other. And as the sun set behind us, casting a beautiful orange glow over everything around us, I knew that our love was eternal. We may face challenges in the future, but as long as we faced them together, nothing could ever tear us apart.

As the night settled in, we all gathered in the palace for dinner. Callie sat between Xander and me, her little hands reaching for the food on each of our plates. Amara and Wesley sat across from us, chatting and laughing about their day. My mom and Lawrence were on one side of the large table, while Hazel, Larina, Erik, and even Victoria sat on the other.

As we ate, we talked about everything and nothing at the same time. Our conversations ranged from the mundane to the exciting, but no matter what we talked about, it always ended in laughter. We may have been rulers of two kingdoms, but we never forgot to enjoy the simple things in life.

After dinner, Xander and I put Callie to bed before retiring to our own room. We lay in bed, our bodies entwined, as we talked about our future plans. As Xander drifted off to sleep, I lay there, staring up at the ceiling and thinking about everything that had brought us to this moment.

I couldn't help but feel a twinge of guilt as I thought about the past. The sacrifices we had made, the people we had hurt and lost.

But then Xander shifted in his sleep, pulling me closer to him, and the guilt faded away. We had made mistakes, but we had learned from them, and our love had only grown stronger as a result.

As I drifted off to sleep, I knew that whatever challenges the future held, we would face them together. And I knew that our love was eternal, just like the moon that shone outside our window.

Acknowledgements

Rachel, thank you for being an amazing editor and friend. I loved hearing your thoughts and theories as you read it for the first time and your comments always have me cackling.

Syd, thanks for always helping me with my blurbs and for being a fantastic developmental editor. Every time I feel like a scene or even the book in general needs a little something more you always help find the best way to add more.

Thank you so much to all my incredible friends and family who have been there for me and helped support me through this amazing journey. I would especially like to thank my mom, Stephanie, Kamarah, Abigail, Rachel, and Syd. I love having some many amazing friends to help me when I am stuck or in my head.

To Celin, you always find a way to make each cover truly amazing. I wasn't sure how we would pull this one off, but of course, you did. It is absolutely stunning and may even be my favourite for the series. Thank you.

Author note

Thank you so much to all my amazing readers, I couldn't have done any of this without your love and support and I truly hope you enjoyed this reading journey as much as I have and that you found this a satisfying ending to these character's journeys… at least for now.

ABOUT THE AUTHOR

Danielle M. Hill is an author and storyteller based in a small town in southern Ontario, Canada. Her stories are drama filled, swoon worthy, and magical that transport readers to new worlds and introduce them to unforgettable characters.

Danielle has been writing since she was a young girl, and her passion for storytelling has only grown stronger over the years. Her debut novel, A Kingdom of Sun and Shadow, was born out of a desire to create a world that readers could escape to and get lost in.

Danielle is a stay at home mom to her daughter and dog. When she's not writing, she enjoys reading, watching Marvel movies, anime, and binge watching TV shows.

Danielle M. Hill is thrilled to share her stories with readers around the world and hopes that her books will bring joy, entertainment, and inspiration to all who read them.

To learn more about Danielle and her books, visit

www.daniellehillwrties.ca

Also by Danielle M. Hill

Young Adult

Twingenuity series:

A Kingdom of Sun and Shadow

The Heir of Magic and Moonlight

The Queens of Prophecy and Power

Stand alone:

Quest for Love

New Adult

Stand alone:

From Steel and Stone